ONE UNHAPPY HORSE

C. S. Adler

Clarion Books
New York

With thanks to Mary Ann Adamcin, ranch owner
and lover of quarter horses extraordinaire. She cared
enough to patiently correct the horse-related material
in this book to make sure the author got it right.

Thanks also to my daughter-in-law, Karen Adler,
whose veterinary medicine expertise I drew on.

Clarion Books
a Houghton Mifflin Company imprint
215 Park Avenue South, New York, NY 10003
Copyright © 2001 by C. S. Adler

The text was set in 13.5-point Garamond.
Designed by Sarah Hokanson.

For information about permission
to reproduce selections from this book,
write to Permissions, Houghton Mifflin Company,
215 Park Avenue South, New York, NY 10003.

www.houghtonmifflinbooks.com

Printed in the USA.

Library of Congress Cataloging-in-Publication Data
Adler, C.S. (Carole S.)
One unhappy horse / C.S. Adler.
Summary: Things are difficult for twelve-year-old Jan and her mother after her
father's death, and when it turns out that her beloved horse needs an operation,
Jan reluctantly gets money from an elderly woman whom she has befriended.
ISBN 0-618-04912-6
[1. Horses—Fiction. 2. Mothers and daughters—Fiction. 3. Old age—Fiction.
4. Friendship—Fiction.] I. Title.

PZ7.A26145 Ho 2000
[Fic]—dc21   00-025907

QUM 10 9 8 7 6 5 4 3 2 1

EXTENSION

To James Cross Giblin,
the wonderful editor who has given me so many
years of unwavering support and wise guidance

CHAPTER ONE

It was hot, over a hundred, even though it was early October. Jan rode Dove toward the shade of the cottonwood trees growing along the wash on the southern border of the ranch. But they hadn't gone more than a few hundred feet before Dove started limping again. Jan slipped off his back and bent down to examine his right front leg. Mom had said that Dove might have a stone bruise, but nothing appeared to be wrong.

"If that's all it is, you're sure taking a long time to heal," Jan told her horse. He had been standing as if he were rooted in the corner of his pipe corral in the shade of the mesquite tree for a week now. Normally, Dove kept himself in motion most of the day.

"You hurting, tall, brown, and handsome?" Jan asked him.

He snorted softly against her shoulder as she laid her cheek against his and combed his reddish brown mane with her fingers. His hair was much the same color as hers. She could still hear Dad's words when he'd given Dove to her five years earlier. "I picked him because he looks like you, Jan. Both long-boned graceful. And you got the same look in your eyes, like you were wanting something."

Now Dad was gone, and the only relief Jan could find from the pain of her loss was being with Dove. Her horse understood her in some unspoken way that no one else did. Certainly not Mom, who understood nothing but work. Mom had closed so tightly into herself this past year that she barely seemed to notice she still had a daughter. Jan suspected she knew the choice Mom would have made if she'd had to pick between losing her husband or her child.

"All right, Dove. I'll put you back in your corral so you can rest some more," Jan said.

She turned her head so as not to see the main house as they walked past it. That house had been home her whole life until Mom had sold it last spring after Dad's accident. A man running a red light at a major Tucson intersection had sideswiped Dad's old pickup truck and killed him instantly. Jan still hadn't recovered from the shock of losing him when Mom moved them into the casita. That was the bunkhouse where a wrangler had stayed when the ranch had been so busy that they could afford hired help. Back then Dad and Mom had not only boarded and trained horses but also given trail rides and riding lessons. Back then—when Dad was alive and they'd been happy.

The casita was so tiny that Jan and her mother couldn't move without bumping into each other. They slept in the same bed, and, as Jan had confided to Dove, Mom kept her awake with her snoring. Besides, no matter how hard they scrubbed the tin shower stall in the bathroom, it still smelled.

The main house had been renovated and turned into River Haven, an assisted living home for a handful of old folks who couldn't quite manage on their own. With a glance, Jan checked the corner window of the bedroom that had been hers. Yes, the blinds were down. They were always down, as if whoever lived there now was some kind of sunlight-hating mole. It angered Jan that people who couldn't even enjoy a little Arizona sunshine should be living in the place that was rightly hers.

Dove stopped to nibble at a tuft of long grass growing in the dirt road. Jan waited for him patiently. If she were riding him, she wouldn't let him graze, but why be strict while they were walking? She stroked his neck. His hide felt sweaty.

"You're hot, but you wouldn't complain, would you, Dove? Not like me, huh?"

Dove had turned his ears her way and was listening patiently. He was a good listener, Dove was. Jan tugged at his lead line to set him moving again. Usually, his sleek, smooth-muscled gait was a joy to watch. He lifted his legs high and held his head up. Now it worried Jan to feel him heaving along beside her on the dirt road that bisected the ranch. He was barely using the tip of his right front foot for balance. She winced as he gave an odd little groan and stumbled for no reason.

"Is something wrong with that pretty horse?" a high voice called.

Jan looked back and found a doll-size old lady with curly white hair coming up behind her.

"His foot hurts him," Jan said. She suspected this could be one of the people from the assisted living house.

"Well, that's too bad. I hope he gets better soon. I'm Mattie," the sweet-faced woman said.

Jan mumbled her own name in return, and the woman continued, "You didn't happen to see an old lady in a house-dress and slippers go by, did you? She slipped out on us again, and I— Oh, my!" Mattie's hands went to her crinkled cheeks.

Jan followed her horrified gaze to the main road, which ran past the entrance to the ranch. The road was so heavily trafficked that few people risked walking along it, but now there was a woman right smack in the middle of it.

Both Jan and Mattie screamed as the woman on the road wavered and was nearly sideswiped by boards hanging out of the back of a wide-bodied truck.

"Sadie, you come back here!" Mattie yelled. She tottered a few steps toward the road.

Jan said, "I'll get her." She dropped Dove's lead line, confident he would stay put, and sprinted diagonally across a field of prickery creosote bushes and weeds. Still running, she ducked under the rail fence beside the road. Meanwhile the woman had wandered into the eastbound lane. Mistake. A speeding car swerved to pass her. It honked madly but didn't stop.

Jan ran onto the road. She grabbed the woman's skeletal arm and pulled her back onto the shoulder. "You're going to get killed," she said.

This person was older than anyone Jan had ever been near. Her white hair grew in sparse threads from her pink scalp, and her skin hung loose on the narrow bones of her face. She looked like a witch. But her eyes had a mischievous glint as she cackled, "Can't catch me. I'm the gingerbread boy." She had on a thin cotton housedress and fuzzy pink scuffs and wasn't carrying even so much as a purse.

"Here, take my hand. I'll get you back," Jan said.

"You know where I live?"

"Did you come from there?" Jan pointed toward the main house.

The woman cocked her head and grinned at Jan. "They lock the door," she confided, "but I can get out." Her laughter was girlish.

Jan slowed her steps to match the old woman's shuffle as she led her back toward the house. It took a while before they caught up with Mattie, who was standing at Dove's head telling him what a good boy he was to be waiting there so patiently.

"It's okay," Jan told Mattie proudly. "He's trained to stay ground-hitched."

"Isn't he something!" Mattie said.

Jan kept steering her charge back toward the main house.

"What's my name?" the lost woman asked Jan slyly as they progressed at a frustrating turtle speed.

"I don't know. What is it?" Jan asked.

"*You* know," the woman said confidently and patted Jan's arm with her free hand. "You're my granddaughter."

"No, I'm not." Jan couldn't imagine being kin to this person, who seemed more apparition than human.

Near the screened-in ramada at the front entrance of the house, Mattie finally rejoined them. "Thank you, honey," she told Jan. "You saved her life. Now I've got to get her back inside before they find out she ran off again." Mattie took the wanderer's hand.

"Hurry, Sadie," she said. "You know how mad they get when you take off." She led Sadie onto the ramada.

Through the glass top of the front door, Jan could see some white-haired people seated in the living room. None of them seemed to be moving to open the door, though Mattie was waving her hand at them. Jan glanced back at Dove. She was curious to see what would happen next, but Dove couldn't stand out in the hot sun forever.

All at once the front door was opened by another ancient woman. This one was tall, thin, and dignified. "Get in quick," she said.

6

Mattie and Sadie followed her into the living room, but Jan saw a younger woman in a white uniform with dark hair slicked back in a ponytail approaching. The uniformed woman was shaking her head disapprovingly.

Jan shook her own head to free herself of a sensation of unreality. She felt as if she'd just participated in a drama staged by aliens. These old people were that different from anyone else she knew.

Dove had to walk only a couple of hundred feet more to his corral after she reclaimed him, but standing seemed to have worsened his limp. "It's got to be more than a stone bruise," Jan told him when she finally had him back in his corral. Resolutely, she marched off to find her mother.

Mom was in the main ring putting their prime boarder through his paces. The black horse was supposed to be exercised daily. Usually it was Mom, and not the horse's teenage owner, who took care of him. "They pay me well to do it," Mom said whenever Jan sounded off in disgust about how anybody could neglect such a beautiful animal.

"So how's Dove doing?" Mom asked from the middle of the ring where she was guiding the prime boarder on the lunge line.

"Bad. So bad an old lady from the main house noticed."

"Well, we'll give it another week, Jan."

"Another *week?* Mom! Please call the vet tomorrow."

Mom sighed. "I suppose we could try Dove on anti-inflammatory pills. I've still got some Bute."

7

"You're not a vet. I mean, I know you're good with horses, but you're not a vet, Mom. Why won't you ask Dr. Foster to come look at Dove?"

Mom gave her a look that was as close to a rebuke as she ever got. "Your father used to say time was the best healer," she said as she revolved patiently to guide the black horse around the inside of the ring.

Jan bit her trembling lip. Dad had said that, true enough. But he'd never have let Dove suffer this long. "Dad wouldn't worry about a vet bill when it came to Dove."

Turning to face her, Mom said evenly, "No, your father never worried about paying bills. And he left us a drawerful of unpaid ones when he died."

This was news to Jan, something her mother had never mentioned. "Probably Dad just didn't have a chance to sit down and do them," Jan said. She'd never heard her mother criticize her father before.

"Maybe," Mom said. "But there wasn't any money to pay them with, either."

"Is that why you sold our house? To pay off bills?"

"I had to," Mom said.

"But banks loan you money when you need it, don't they?" Jan asked. She knew Mom hated to be beholden to anybody for anything. She suspected her mother would rather starve than ask for a loaf of bread. "You didn't have to sell the house in such a hurry. You could have borrowed the money to pay what we owed."

"There were overdue bank loans in that drawer, big ones," Mom said. "I did my best, Jan. If I hadn't sold the house, we would have lost the whole ranch."

"Maybe we'd be better off," Jan said bitterly. "Then I wouldn't have to keep being reminded of how it used to be back when Dad was alive and people knew how to laugh around here."

A twitch in Mom's gaunt cheeks was her only reaction. Patiently, she said, "If we'd sold off the whole ranch, what would I do for a living? The only work I'm good at is with horses. Besides, you couldn't keep Dove if we didn't have a place for him."

"I know what we can do," Jan said, buoyed by the idea that had suddenly come to her. "We can use my savings account to pay the vet."

"I wouldn't be so quick to spend that if I were you. There could be an emergency—"

"Mom!" Jan cried. "This *is* an emergency."

"We'll give it another week," her mother repeated quietly.

Jan turned on her boot heel and stalked off to Dove's corral. She gave him a good rubdown and left him groaning with pleasure with his head eye-deep in Bermuda hay. "Those anti-inflammatory pills'll make you feel better fast," she told him.

And if they didn't? Mom was so stubborn, so hard. Nothing moved her now that Dad was gone. It was like Dad was the only thing she had ever cared about. Not that she'd shed a tear for him. "There's no use in all that crying," Mom had said to Jan last summer. "Tears won't bring him back."

They wouldn't, but at least Jan still had Dove. What if something was very wrong with him? No, Jan told herself. She couldn't lose her father *and* the big house that she'd grown up in *and* her horse all in one year. Life couldn't be *that* unfair.

CHAPTER TWO

Jan had never liked going to school. Even when Dad had seen to it that she was outfitted with the right clothes, she hadn't felt as if she belonged. Dad had said her attachment to Dove was the problem. He'd teased her, saying if he'd known how much space the horse would take in her life, he wouldn't have given her Dove for her seventh birthday.

That had allowed Mom to jibe, "I told you we couldn't afford a pet horse on this ranch."

"It's not the money," Dad had said, "but I don't want the horse making our girl into a loner."

"I'm not a loner," Jan had protested. "I just like being with Dove and you guys best." She didn't care about TV programs and computer games and shopping malls and team sports the way the other kids did. Even the few who loved horses talked either about showing them or about rodeo.

As far as the lessons part of school, learning was a chore to get through. And now that Dove had a problem, Jan was having a hard time concentrating. She sat in social studies class while the teacher, Mr. Coss, droned on about the importance of topographical maps, but she didn't register a word he said. She was wondering if the Bute tablets that she'd mixed with bran and that Dove had lapped up so eagerly that morning would work. Dove had nickered, as if to ask her where she was going when she left him, and she'd nearly missed the bus to go back to hug him. It had seemed to her that the hot surge of her love should help heal him. Surely, its power had to have some use.

"Soon you're going to feel so good that we can go cantering down the road," she'd promised him. Then the driver had honked impatiently and she'd had to sprint.

One day—that's the time she'd give the Bute to cure Dove. If it didn't, she'd remind Mom that Dad wouldn't have hesitated to call the vet. "Life's too short to be economizing all the time," Dad had always said when Mom objected to his buying something. Well, he'd been right about life being short because he was only thirty-six when he died. "My girls," Dad had called his wife and daughter in a voice syrupy with love and pride. He'd been the center of their lives, the only one who could make Mom relax enough to enjoy herself, the only one who could make her smile.

By lunchtime, Jan had chewed her lip until it was sore and slightly swollen. Besides, she wasn't hungry. Even pizza didn't seem appealing today. She bought milk and an apple and went in search of an empty seat in the noisy cafeteria.

She felt exposed standing there alone with her backpack on her back and her hands full. It wasn't just that her jeans had the wrong label and she was wearing an old shirt of her father's with the sleeves rolled up instead of a fashionable stretchy-fabric top. It wasn't just that she was too tall and long-jawed and thin. What made her an outsider here was that she had no close friend among these kids she'd been going to school with since first grade. The embarrassment of being solitary made her think of taking refuge in the computer room. Kids could spend lunch hour there but not eat. Jan was considering ditching her apple and milk so she could go when someone called her name.

"Come sit with us," Brittany hailed her. Brittany was a people magnet. She collected kids around her wherever she was and had more friends than the old woman in the shoe had children. Jan liked her, but she had learned not to expect much from Brittany. The girl had to divide her time and affection up into too many little pieces.

Today, though, Jan was grateful for even a small piece. "Thanks," she said to Brittany and fitted her narrow hips onto the bench at the end of Brittany's crowded table. Blended into the crowd at last, Jan relaxed. All she had to do now was listen.

For once everyone at the table was female. They were talking about boys and how stupid they could be.

"Do you have a boyfriend?" the girl sitting next to Jan asked her. The personal question surprised Jan because she didn't know this small, intense, freckle-faced girl who was new in their school.

"No boyfriend. Not me," Jan said.

"Did you ever have a boyfriend?" the girl persisted.

"She has a horse," smart-mouth Barbara said from across the table. "They're going steady."

"Oh," said the girl, leaning toward Jan. "I had a horse for a while, but I got tired of getting up early to take care of it before school. Does your father make you do that?"

"No," Jan said. She wasn't about to confide to a stranger that her father was dead. To distract her, Jan asked quickly, "Do you ride much?"

"Well, I used to ride in Connecticut. That's where I lived," the girl answered. "But that was English saddle. You know, posting and that stuff? I've never ridden western style."

"It's easy," Jan said. "You just sit the saddle and put pressure on your toes instead of with your knees."

"So what's your horse like?" the girl asked.

Jan stiffened and answered shortly, "He's lame right now."

"Is that why you're so grumpy?" The girl asked it with a smile that took the sting off her words.

Jan didn't know what to answer. She took a bite of her apple and munched, fixing her eyes on the table. The girl

14

inched away from her then and turned to face the other end of the table where they were talking about a rock star who was coming to Tucson. Jan felt bad. The new girl had just been trying to be friendly. If only she had her father's knack with people! "Nothing to it," Dad would say. "Just smile, and most folks will smile right back." She hadn't smiled. If she had, would the girl have become her friend? Probably not. The ranch was too isolated. Besides, she didn't have time for a friend now with Dove sick.

Dove's head came up expectantly when he saw Jan coming toward his corral that afternoon. He nickered, tossing his head and showing his teeth in his funny smiling way.

"So did the medicine work?" Jan asked him. She patted his neck and knuckled him under the ear the way he liked. Taking her time about it, she went about cleaning up the dirty shavings and shoveling in fresh.

Dove butted her in the rear end with his head, nearly knocking her into the soiled shavings she was piling into the wheelbarrow. It had been a favorite trick of his when she first got him, and she'd worked hard to break him of it. But now she was glad to find him so frisky. "If you're feeling so good, how about a little exercise?" Jan asked.

The sun blazed in a pale sapphire sky, scouring the desert with its heat even though Halloween was only a few weeks off. Jan was happy because Dove finally seemed to be walking better. She decided to try mounting him and see how he did with her on his back. If she kept to the dirt road inside the ranch and stopped when he showed signs of tiring, it should be all right.

She was riding Dove bareback, leaning over his neck to tell him how glad she was that he was fit again, when she spotted the tiny curly-haired lady who had helped her rescue the wanderer yesterday. The lady—what had she said her name was? Mattie? Yes, that was it. Mattie was walking with another old woman as tall and thin as a crane. Jan had seen people from the home out walking before and had deliberately avoided them. Today she meant to pass them on the opposite side of the road. Should she say hi since Mattie wasn't quite a stranger anymore? But if she did, and Mattie didn't recall her from yesterday, it would be embarrassing.

While Jan was still trying to make up her mind whether to pass in silence or not, Mattie stopped short and grabbed her companion's arm to halt her.

"Look there! It's the girl who saved Sadie," Mattie said. Her high, quick voice carried easily in the still air. "Our hero—or is it heroine? Heroine, I guess, seeing she's a girl. Right, Amelia?"

"Correct," Amelia said. She stood statue-still in the middle of the road, eyes aimed straight ahead.

"Is that pretty horse yours, dear?" Mattie asked Jan. "I've forgotten your name. When you get old as me, you're lucky you can remember your own name. Right, Amelia?"

16

"I remember fine," Amelia said. "I just can't see anymore."

"Amelia's legally blind," Mattie said, "but she can see her way to the table for meals just as good as you and me."

"Hmm," Amelia said without much heat.

"My name is Jan. Jan Wright. And my horse's name is Dove," Jan said.

"Wright? That's the name of the family that owned this ranch," Amelia said.

"We still own the working part of it," Jan was quick to point out.

Mattie had approached Dove and was stroking his neck. He allowed her touch while he waited patiently for Jan's next signal.

"Why, was it you, then, who carved your name inside of our closet door?" Mattie asked Jan. "I saw that name there, and I remember thinking, I bet some girl wanted us to know this was her room."

Jan felt a blush coming on. Luckily her skin was tanned enough to hide it. She remembered defiantly carving her name on the door the day Mom told her that their house had been sold. "Yes, that was me," she admitted.

"So where do you live now, honey?"

"In the casita." Jan swiveled her slim hips and pointed back over her shoulder at the tiny building with its postage-stamp ramada.

"That itty bitty place?" Mattie said. "My, you must be mad at us for taking over your nice big house."

Jan felt her cheeks heating up again, but she mumbled, "I'm not mad at you."

Mattie shook her head doubtfully. "I guess I would be."

Amelia said nothing.

"Want to pet this horse, Amelia?" Mattie asked. "I used to have a pretty, mahogany-colored quarter horse like him when I was a girl in Mississippi, you know."

"You told me," Amelia said dryly. "More than once."

Unfazed, Mattie turned back to Jan to say, "My daddy got me a horse for my fourth birthday, and was I ever wild about him! Right from the start, when I was too small to ride him."

"Wild about your daddy or your horse?" Amelia asked sharply.

Mattie's answer bypassed the sarcasm. "Both. I was wild about both. You know that horse of mine lived until I got married? Then I had to leave him behind on my mother's place, and he up and died. Mama said he missed me. But I don't know. He was old by then."

"So are we old," Amelia said, "and we're not dying."

"Some of us are getting pretty close, Amelia." Mattie turned to look up at Jan and said confidentially, "You know Sadie, that woman you rescued yesterday?"

"Yes," Jan said.

"Well, we didn't get away with hiding that she'd wandered off again. This morning they took her off to the nursing home, that one in the middle of Tucson." Mattie shook her head sadly.

"Was she sick?" Jan asked.

"Just up here." Mattie pointed to her head.

Jan felt a cold ripple down her spine. How awful, she thought, to be carted off against your will just because you got lost easily. "Will she come back soon?" she asked.

"Next step after the nursing home's the grave," Amelia said. She still hadn't moved from her position in the middle of the road.

"Well," Mattie said, "at least they don't have us yet, Amelia. Come on. I best get you out of the sun before you get heatstroke." Mattie took the tall woman's hand and said to Jan, "She won't wear a hat. I always tell her when we go for a walk, she should wear a hat, but she won't." Mattie laughed. "Stubborn, that's what Amelia is."

"That's what all old people are. Keeps us alive," Amelia said. She took a step in the direction Mattie had turned her, back toward the main house.

They would have to walk down the dirt road a quarter of a mile and then cross a field to get into the desert garden at the back of the house, where one could sit on the patio out of the hot afternoon sun. Jan missed the patio almost as much as she missed having her own room. She missed the cave-like cool inside the thick walls of the baked-brick ranch house, which hugged the ground and resisted the heat of the day. She missed the smells from the kitchen when Dad was cooking dinner, something he was better at than Mom. Life had been good when they lived in that house.

Before the two old ladies had taken more than a few steps, Mattie looked back over her shoulder at Jan and Dove. Her smile was bright as she said, "Come visit sometime, honey. I'll show you a picture of my Laddie-lee. That's what I named my horse when I was four. He was big, like your horse, but he had a white blaze between his eyes, and—Did I tell you he saved my life one time?"

"Let the girl be," Amelia chided her. "She's got more to do than listen to your old stories."

"Now, Amelia, you just feel that way because you've heard them all." Mattie turned toward Jan again. "Amelia and I share a room. We're the only two in our house that share. The others all have their own room. . . . But we don't mind it that much, do we, Amelia?"

"It must be getting close to suppertime," Amelia said.

She started forward again and Mattie followed, offering Amelia her arm. Over her shoulder, Mattie called out to Jan, "Come by anytime, honey. We *love* visitors, especially pretty young things like you. Bye, now." She waved and then concentrated on guiding Amelia.

She'd never step inside that house again, Jan thought. She'd hate being a guest in her own home and trying to make conversation with those women. What could she possibly have to say to them? They had nothing in common. But that Mattie did have a sweet face. She might have been pretty once, though it was hard to imagine she had ever been young. Of course—Jan smiled to herself as she thought it—she wouldn't have to worry much about having to talk if Mattie were there.

Jan continued riding Dove slowly along the dirt road, but a few minutes after her encounter with Mattie and Amelia, Dove stumbled. Not that there was anything in the road for him to stumble on—his knee just seemed to buckle under him. And then he stumbled again. He wasn't better, Jan realized. It had been wishful thinking on her part to think the anti-inflammatory pills had worked so fast. She slid off his back and turned him around to walk him home.

"I'm sorry, Dove. I shouldn't have tried to ride you. You hurt, don't you? I wish you could tell me what's wrong."

She would get out her bankbook as soon as they got home and slap it down on the kitchen table and tell Mom she had to get a vet to look at Dove *now*.

CHAPTER THREE

When Jan returned to the casita, Mom was on the phone trying to convince a man that he still had to pay his horse's boarding bill even if he didn't want the horse anymore. She wasn't sounding very persuasive. Dad had always been the one to charm people into paying. Better wait until suppertime to confront her mother, Jan decided.

She began as soon as Mom finished microwaving their frozen pizza. "Mom, Dove's worse, not better. You said—"

"I said we need to give him time to heal himself. You only gave him the Bute this morning," Mom interrupted her.

"But I just know he's got more wrong with him than a stone bruise. I want to pay the vet to look at him."

Mom swallowed and surprised Jan by saying, "All right, if your money's burning a hole in your pocket—Dr. Foster's coming tomorrow to see a boarder's horse for a bad infection. I'll ask her to look at Dove while she's here."

"Thanks," Jan said with relief. She wasn't about to question why Mom had suddenly given in. She was just glad her mother had.

They finished their pizza slices in a silence that made Jan aware of every chewing and swallowing noise. Dad's cheery dinner-table conversation used to cover up such noises. Jan looked at her mother's tired face and tried, "So how was your day, Mom?"

"Same as always." Mom's eyes met Jan's. She swallowed and offered up in return the question that Dad had always put. "How was school?"

"Fine. I sat with some kids at lunch and met this new girl. She was friendly, but I didn't get her name."

Mom nodded and dropped her eyes to her pizza again. Subject ended. Jan tried a new one. "I keep bumping into this old lady who moved into our house." Briefly, Jan described how she'd met Mattie and how the wanderer they'd rescued had ended up in a nursing home.

"That's too bad," Mom said. "Poor lady."

Jan finished her iced tea. She left the crusts of her two pizza slices on her plate, while Mom chewed away patiently on her own crusts. Mom's family hadn't had any food to waste, she had told Jan more than once.

"Mattie's one of the ladies that get assisted, I guess." Jan was thinking of the term "assisted living facility," which she'd heard applied to their old house. "But I don't see why she needs help. She seems fine."

"You like her? I thought you were mad that old people took over our place."

"Well, I was, but I sort of like Mattie, even though she's ancient. . . . I've never known anyone really old."

"Me, neither," Mom said. "Nobody lives long in my family."

"There's Dad's mother," Jan said. "But she dyes her hair and she married that man after Grandpa died and moved to England with him. That doesn't seem old."

Her mother gave a wry smile. "Age is supposed to bring wisdom. In your grandmother's case—" Mom broke off, unwilling to speak outright ill of anyone.

"Grandma's too bossy," Jan said because she was glad to agree with her mother on something. "She's so sure she knows how everybody should live."

"She thought your father made some bad choices," Mom said. "And she may be right."

"What do you mean?" Jan asked.

"Well, this ranch. I'm working as hard as I can and we still can't seem to pull up even, much less get a penny ahead."

Mom's eyes were so sad that Jan felt an urge to comfort her. Dad would have slung an arm around his wife's shoulders now. He would have said something about things getting better. But Jan and her mother avoided touching each other. And what could Jan promise that wouldn't be false? The best she could offer was, "I'll get up early tomorrow and help you with the horses, Mom."

"That's okay," her mother said. "I can manage the twenty boarders we've got."

"But I want to help you," Jan said.

"Well, if you wake up in time, and you feel like it, that would be nice." Mom gave Jan a shy smile. Jan smiled back. It struck her that Mom had lost even more than she had when Dad died. He'd been the only one Mom could talk to, as well as her business partner and beloved husband. And Mom didn't even have Dove to fill in for him.

"Do you hate it that we don't live in the big house anymore?" Jan asked.

Her mother considered for so long that Jan thought she wasn't going to answer. Finally, she said, "I hate it that your father died before me. My parents died in their forties, so I was sure I'd go first."

"Well, you'd better not die in your forties. I'd be a total orphan then," Jan said.

Her mother's smile didn't reach her eyes. "I'm not going anywhere soon that I know of," she said.

As usual, Mom got busy with her paperwork after dinner. Jan washed and dried their two dishes and glasses, careful not to waste precious water. She was wiping the table when she realized that her mother hadn't exactly answered her question. Or had she? Probably what she had meant by her comment on dying was that Dad had been the most important person in her life. Next would probably come Jan and the horses. The house would be down at the bottom of Mom's list. She'd never cared about domestic things. A beautiful saddle had always excited her more than any couch or dish or chair.

And what was on *her* list, Jan wondered. Mom and Dove . . . and then? Then nothing. She wished she hadn't been so awkward when that new girl tried to be friendly.

At lunchtime in school the next day, Brittany grabbed Jan's shirttail as she passed with her tray. "Sit with us. There's still room," Brittany said.

Jan squeezed in at the table and found herself next to the new girl again. "Hi," Jan greeted her with a grin.

"Hi. How's your horse?"

"I don't know. The vet's going to examine him today."

"Uh-huh," the new girl nodded and looked away.

Now what? Jan threw out the first question that came to mind. "Do you have a grandmother?"

"Well, sure," the girl answered, as if she expected everyone to have a grandmother. "Mine lives with us. She takes care of the house and my brother and me so my mom can do her volunteer jobs."

"Boy!" Barbara said, joining in the conversation uninvited. "That's pretty good. I mean, a grandmother who does something useful. All my grandma does is take ballroom dancing lessons and shop for sequined gowns and fancy shoes."

"Are you talking about grandmothers?" Brittany asked from where she presided at midtable.

"Yes," Barbara said. "I was just telling them mine's a dancing maniac." That got a laugh, which seemed to satisfy Barbara.

"My grandma travels all the time and sends me neat things from all over the world," Brittany said.

"So what about your grandmother?" the new girl asked Jan.

"I don't know her very well," Jan said. "She lives in England. On my birthday she sends a check. But I never get to see her."

"Better than my grandma," Barbara said. "On my birthday she gives me something awful that I can't wear, like a vest with cats painted all over it."

"What's wrong with that?" the new girl asked. "I like cats."

"Pink and purple cats with evil grins?"

Everybody laughed.

The conversation moved on to Halloween costumes and whether they were too old to go trick-or-treating. Jan had never dressed up and gone trick-or-treating. The two houses within walking distance of hers were forlorn places whose owners wouldn't have known what to do about a trick or treater at their door.

She wondered if the vet had come yet. What if Dr. Foster said she didn't have time to look at Dove? Worse yet, what if she found something awful wrong with him?

Closing her eyes, Jan set herself to wondering something

neutral. Like how old Mattie was. Mattie and the other old lady with her, Amelia—they didn't sound like the grandmothers these girls had been talking about: lively grandmothers who were active and traveled and had boyfriends. Mattie and Amelia were past grandmother age. "Come see us," Mattie had said. No, Jan wouldn't go into the house that used to be hers. It would be too awkward and depressing. There might be other people in it, like the wanderer whose mind didn't work right anymore. Being that old would be awful. It would be better to die before needing assistance with living.

Jan sighed and scolded herself for being morbid. Wonder about something else now, she told herself. Immediately, she returned to worrying about what the vet could have found wrong with Dove.

CHAPTER FOUR

Jan rushed off the school bus and ran past Dove, who was standing at the far side of his corral waiting to greet her, without even stopping to say hello. She found her mother in the tack room at the far end of the barn. "What did the vet say?"

Mom heaved a saddle blanket onto the top of a stack and turned to face Jan. Bad news was written in every line of her long, thin face. "She said she'd have to come back with the x-ray machine to tell for sure, but it's more than a stone bruise."

"So when will she do the x-rays?"

"I told her I'd think about it and call her."

"Mom! Call her right now. We can pay for the x-rays. I've got nearly two hundred dollars in my savings account."

"But what if Dove needs an operation? Where would we get the money for that?" Mom asked.

"I don't know. I guess we could borrow it," Jan said. "You paid back the bank, didn't you? After you sold the main house? So we can borrow from them again."

Mom's face was all hungry hollows today. "Didn't you hear me say that we're barely breaking even? We can't borrow what we can't pay back."

"There's got to be a way," Jan said stubbornly.

"Well, if I could get another boarder, maybe that'd help some," Mom admitted.

"But where would you put another horse?"

Mom shrugged. "This tack room used to be a corner stall. If I closed in the shed near the barn with some Sheetrock and siding, we could move the tack out there."

Obviously, Mom had been thinking about the problem. Jan was so grateful that her voice rang with enthusiasm as she said, "Great. I'll help you."

Her mother squinted at her. "You sure you want to spend your money on x-rays?"

"I'm positive."

"But, Jan, an operation could cost thousands of dollars. If your horse needs one, we'd still be short a whole lot of money, even with a boarder. And you're not going to like my other idea of how to bring in some money."

"What is it? Tell me." Jan braced herself. Her mother didn't usually build up to bad news. She just came right out with it, which Jan preferred to Dad's way of hiding hard truths as if Jan weren't strong enough to take them.

"Of course, we really don't need to think about it yet," Mom said. She eyed Jan guiltily.

"You're not going to say we should eat less?" Jan joked. Neither of them ate much and they never ate out. "Or buy fewer clothes?" Mom never bought anything, and the only new clothes Jan had started school with this fall were a pair of discount-store jeans and a shirt. "I already said I was willing to go to the thrift shop. You were the one who was too proud to do that."

"No, this is something I heard about. And you'd have to wait until Dove's well to do it, anyway."

Jan pressed her lips together to control her impatience. "What, Mom?" she repeated.

"It's called leasing," Mom said. "You find someone who wants his or her own horse but can't afford to buy one, and you go partners on your horse with the person."

"Share Dove?" Jan couldn't believe Mom would suggest such a thing. "Let someone else ride my horse?"

"*And* help take care of him *and* pay his expenses. It wouldn't hurt Dove, and it would bring in money."

Jan turned her back on her mother. Her heart was racing fast enough to burst out of her chest. "No," she said. "No, I couldn't do that." Then she ran to Dove's corral and threw herself at him. He backed up a couple of steps before he steadied and nuzzled her as she hugged him. She would have leaped on his back and galloped away as far as he could go if he had been able to run—but he wasn't. Instead, she clung to him until the anger began to seep out of her.

31

Her mother would never suggest she share Dove with anyone if Dad were alive. Dad would figure a way to help Dove that wouldn't involve renting him out to some stranger. He'd find a dozen bright possibilities where Mom saw none.

As if he sensed her misery, Dove kept nudging her. He backpedaled in a circle on his three good legs, barely letting the tip of the right front hoof touch the ground. His ears whisked one way and then the other in confusion. Jan began to feel guilty about upsetting him. To comfort them both, she got his brush out of the barn and began to groom him.

Dove stuck his tongue out to lick her neck, but she told him, "Stop that." He'd tried to lick any bare skin within reach when they first got him. Dad had warned her to break him of the habit because licking led to biting, and even a playful nip that wouldn't harm another horse could do damage to a human.

"You know, Dove," she said, "you have it better hanging out here all day than I do going to school. At least you can watch the hawks fly by and smell things in the wind." She touched his sore leg by accident, but he gave no sign that it hurt him.

"Hello, there!" The high-pitched greeting came from the road. Jan turned to see Mattie calling and waving at her. "That's a pretty horse you've got there. Is he yours?"

"Yes," Jan said. She frowned, thinking that Mattie had asked her that question before.

"Well, can I come say hi to him?"

"Sure," Jan said. She'd be glad to be distracted.

Mattie was alone this time. Her pink plaid pants matched her solid pink blouse, and her straw hat had a pink ribbon around it. "You look nice," Jan told her when Mattie had crossed the road to the corral area.

"Thanks, honey. I got dressed up for my daughter. She was going to take me out shopping, and I must have bored a hole in the front door watching for her. But just now she called to say she couldn't make it. She's so busy, you know. She's an executive at a big company here in Tucson." Mattie was stroking Dove's neck. He muttered and turned his head into Jan's shoulder as if to ask who this stranger was.

Mattie frowned and stopped in midstroke. "Now, why can't I remember right? My daughter quit that job so she could stay home and be a consultant. A consultant just tells companies what to do, and they pay her good for it. I think that's what she said. It's so she doesn't have to work so hard. But—" Mattie looked at Jan as if Jan might unmuddle her, but Jan couldn't.

"Anyway," Mattie said with renewed cheer, "it's not that my daughter doesn't want to see me. She and I are as close as— Why, once she even sent me a card that said I was her best friend."

"Uh-huh," Jan said.

"Yes," Mattie assured herself. "But she's busy. So I thought I'd take myself for a little walk in the fresh air. And

I'm sure glad I did because here you are, and isn't this nice?" She leaned her cheek against Dove's warm neck.

"The vet looked at Dove's leg today," Jan said. "But she isn't sure what's wrong. She's got to do x-rays."

"X-rays? They did those on my head after the car accident, but they couldn't find anything." Mattie laughed. "I guess that's because there's not much up there to find." She knocked her fist against her skull.

Jan tried to smile, but she couldn't quite manage it.

"Well, don't look so sad," Mattie said. "Whatever's wrong with this big horse can be fixed. He's young, isn't he?"

"Dove's sixteen."

"Oh, that's a good age for a horse. You'll be grown up and married before he's too old to patch up."

"But we don't have any money to get him patched up," Jan said.

"Umm." Mattie frowned and shook her head. "Money's a nasty business, isn't it? I gave all mine over to my daughter so I wouldn't have to think about it. There're always people in trouble and needing help, and I didn't have enough to help everyone. At least, that's what my daughter kept telling me."

Dove dipped his head down and nudged Mattie's shoulder. Although it was a gentle nudge, it nearly knocked her off her feet. Jan scolded him, but Mattie seemed delighted by his acknowledgment of her.

"He likes me!" she cried. "There, big fella. You like me, don't you?" And she reached up to stroke his cheek. "Next

34

time I'm gonna ask Stella for a carrot to bring you," she told Dove, nose to nose with him.

Jan smiled down at Mattie. The woman was so small that she made Jan feel like a giant string puppet, all legs and arms. "How's your friend, the tall one who can't see so well?" Jan asked.

"Amelia? She's fine. But you know, she's not really my friend. We room together because I've got to be economical and share. *She's* got money, but she needs someone with her because of her eyes."

Jan was confused. "You mean, you don't like her?"

"Oh, I like her. I like everybody. But Amelia—she's kind of *sour* about things, you know?"

Jan didn't know, but she was shy about prying. Dad had never hesitated to ask people personal questions, and they'd never seemed to mind his asking. Too bad she wasn't more like her father, she thought. He might have been a spendthrift like Mom claimed, but everybody had loved him. And *he'd* known how to enjoy life.

"Well, now, when are you coming to visit?" Mattie asked. "I want to show you a picture of my old horse."

"Oh, I don't know. Soon, I guess," Jan said evasively.

"Why not right now? You can't ride this fellow, can you?"

"No. But I think I'd better—"

"It won't take long. I'll just show you the picture and you can leave. We're not going to lock you in or anything." Mattie's smile was mischievous. Jan was embarrassed that

35

Mattie had somehow sensed her reluctance to enter her old home.

"Okay," Jan said, because she couldn't think of a polite way out of it.

"Good," Mattie said enthusiastically. "Come on, then." She took Jan's arm as if it belonged to her now. Her small hand went tap-tap, tap-tap against Jan's lean, tanned forearm as they walked through the dry weeds toward the back of the main house.

A wall had been constructed around the patio, which had been lined with a neat row of desert cactus and succulents. A small square of grass had been planted outside the brick patio area. A wide-bodied, white-haired lady sat slumped in a plastic garden chair in the sun there. At her knees was a metal framework with wheels and handles that Jan guessed was to help her walk.

"Hi, there, sugar. You ought to get yourself into the shade before you get heatstroke," Mattie told the lady, who looked up with a vague smile.

Apprehension made Jan's heart pound loudly in her ears when she suddenly found herself in her old house. The sun porch, where she had done her homework sprawled on a daybed, was now neatly decked out as a dining room with handsome carved-wood tables and chairs—two sets of them.

"Here's where we eat," Mattie said unnecessarily. "And this is Stella. She's the manager. She takes the *best* care of us."

Stella was setting the tables. Dressed in a white uniform and sensible white shoes, with her hair slicked back in a ponytail, she looked about Jan's mother's age. It pleased Jan to see Stella reach out and hug Mattie. She wasn't the only one to find the curly-haired lady lovable, it seemed.

"So you finally corralled your young friend, Mattie," Stella said. "I figured you'd persuade her once you put your mind to it."

"She and her family used to own this house," Mattie said.

"You told me. Well, you better show her around and see if she approves of how we fixed it up," Stella said amiably. "Nice to meet you—"

"Jan," Jan provided, since Mattie hadn't introduced her by name.

"Nice to meet you, Jan. Don't you be a stranger, now."

Mattie continued towing Jan into the living room. Jan stiffened herself for the shock of change in what had been so comfortably familiar. The stone fireplace wall was still the same, but the tacky odds and ends of furniture were gone. Instead, there were matching couches and chairs uphol-stered in a pale gray Southwestern design set soothingly against white-painted walls.

"This room looks a whole lot better than when we lived here," Jan said honestly.

"Oh, now, you don't have to say that." Mattie looked around appreciatively. "But I must say it does look nice.

When my daughter first talked about me moving in here, I didn't like it. I'd lived in my own home my whole life, and sharing a room, well— But since the car accident, my head's not right and I get these spells. My daughter says she's afraid to leave me by my lonesome for long. So—" Mattie shrugged and continued cheerily, "Do you have your own room, honey?"

Jan shook her head. "I share with my mother. I had my own room when we lived here."

"Then you know how it is. But you get used to having someone around, don't you? And it's nice to have company." Mattie nodded as if to convince herself. Then she said, "I'd better go see if Amelia's decent before I march you into our bedroom. You wait here a second. Sit down anywhere you like. You can watch TV."

Jan sat on one of the two big sofas across from the giant TV in the corner. It was running without sound, although no one was in the room to watch it besides her. In the casita, Mom often fell asleep watching TV late at night. Then it would sometimes be left on for days until one or the other of them thought to turn it off.

Mattie was back in a minute with a framed picture in her hands. "I'd like you to see what's become of your old bedroom, but Amelia's napping. She spends as much time as she can asleep. Says that's when she's best off. Anyway, we won't bother her. Here." She handed over what was obviously her prize possession, an eight-by-ten picture of a handsome brown quarter horse with a small girl in a cowboy hat atop it.

"That's you?" Jan asked, pointing to the girl.

"Me when I was about seven, and my darling Laddie-lee."

"He looks just like Dove, except for the white on his forehead."

"He does, doesn't he? They both have that proud way of standing with their head up and that sweet look in the eyes."

Jan handed the photo back to Mattie. "Thanks," she said. "I mean, for showing it to me."

"Oh, that's nothing," Mattie said. "I'm just so glad you came to visit. It's good to have a friend close by, isn't it?"

Jan was startled. Was Mattie claiming her as a friend now? The possibility of friendship with this ancient lady hadn't occurred to her. She swallowed. "Well, I guess I'd better—" she began.

"Oh, do you have to go so soon? I could tell you the story of how Laddie-lee saved my life if you've got another minute," Mattie said.

"You'd better watch out," Stella stuck her head in to say. "That Mattie won't let go once she gets an audience."

"You think I talk too much, Stella?" Mattie asked, cocking her head inquiringly.

"Oh, not too much for me, Mattie. But you *are* a good talker."

"I like listening to you," Jan said, quickly before Mattie could feel hurt.

"There, you see. This child doesn't mind me."

"I don't mind you, either," Stella said. "But you'd better tell your story fast. I'm serving supper in five minutes."

It was only five o'clock. "You eat early," Jan said to Mattie.

"That's 'cause most of the ladies here go to bed so early. They sleep all day and go to bed around eight or nine at the latest."

Mattie didn't belong in this place, Jan thought. She had entirely too much energy.

The story, when Jan finally sat down next to Mattie and listened to it, was a good one. It seemed Mattie had been riding her horse along the bank of a creek in Mississippi and had dismounted to poke around in the water when a copperhead dropped out of the tree under which she was standing. It landed at her feet. The snake would have bitten and maybe killed her, except that Laddie-lee screamed, the terrible way only a horse can scream. He immediately attacked the reptile, pounding it to a mush with his hooves.

"Now, he could have just run off, Laddie-lee could have. But he stayed and protected me because he loved me. Isn't that something?" Mattie asked.

"It's great," Jan said.

"Yes, I always thought so. I loved Laddie-lee like he was my family. Well, he *was* my family." Mattie's eyes filled. "I still miss him. I had other horses later, but none like him."

Nothing Mattie had said touched Jan as much as the way

she'd expressed her attachment to her horse. Clearly, despite the difference in their ages, they did have a lot in common.

"Supper, Mattie," Stella said.

Jan got up to leave. "Thanks for the story," she said.

"Plenty more where that came from," Mattie said. "You come back soon, hear?"

Stella followed Jan out the back door to the patio while the women began to take their places at the tables in the dining room.

"You did a good deed stopping by here today," Stella said in a low voice. "She's a sweetheart and lately she's been so lonely."

"But she has a daughter."

Stella sniffed and raised an eyebrow. "Mattie's daughter's been making more promises than she keeps. She hasn't been by here in a month. And when she does come—well, it's hard to believe she could be Mattie's daughter. Anyway, you take care, now." And Stella waved and smiled and backed into the house where the white heads were assembled around the tables and waiting to be served.

The sun was turning the craggy Catalina Mountains red to the north of the ranch. It was getting dark earlier every day. Jan went into the casita and dug her savings-account passbook from the bottom drawer of the small dresser she shared with her mother. There were several years of birthday money in the account, plus what Dad had paid her for doing odd jobs around the ranch. She took the passbook back to the barn and held it out to her mother, who was leading one of the boarders into his stall.

"Would you cash this for me to pay for the x-rays if I sign the withdrawal slip?" Jan asked.

"I can take you to the bank tomorrow after school," Mom said. "Maybe you'll be lucky. Maybe the x-rays'll show that Dove *doesn't* need an operation."

"Maybe," Jan said. But somehow she didn't feel very lucky.

CHAPTER FIVE

Dove was standing under his mesquite tree waiting for her when Jan got home from school the next day. He swished his tail and ducked his head a couple of times to greet her, but he maintained his tripod position.

"Are you trying to turn into a statue, Dove?" Jan asked. She went to the barn for the knotted rope that he loved to play with and wagged it under his nose. Dove sniffed it, but he didn't grab an end of it for an impromptu game of tug-of-war.

"Don't you even want to chew a knot loose?" Jan asked him. Dove used to love to untie knots. He had to be hurting bad if he didn't want to play. To comfort him, she scratched under his chin and smiled at how funny he looked when he wrinkled his muzzle lifting his head for her to reach under it.

"So," she said, "looks like I'm going to buy you some x-rays instead of a new saddle blanket. Well, we can make do with your raggedy old blanket. I'll just fold it so the holes don't bother your back. Luckily, you and I aren't fussy about what we wear, are we?"

He sighed for answer. She combed his mane back with her fingers and told him how handsome he was.

When she finally went in search of her mother, Jan didn't find her in the barn or working in the rings. Most likely, Mom had taken their prime boarder out for a trail ride, Jan told herself. That horse didn't get much attention from his owners, but at least they could afford to pay Mom to exercise and groom him. If all Mom's owners were as rich as the prime boarder's, the ranch would be making a profit. But most people could barely afford the boarding costs, plus the incidentals of shoeing and vet fees. According to Mom, people usually underestimated the expense of horse ownership and didn't realize that buying the horse was the least of it.

Horses were neighing and stomping, impatient to be fed. Jan went to the shed where the bales of alfalfa hay were stacked higher than her head. She swung herself up to the top rank by the rope hanging from a roof beam. From there she rolled a bale down, heaved it into a wheelbarrow, and set off with a pitchfork to shake a flake of hay into each of the hungry horses' feeders. As usual, the Appaloosa grabbed for the hay and dropped most of it before Jan could get it into his feeder. "Piggy," she told him. "Now you'll have to eat it from the ground."

By the time she'd distributed the hay flakes, Mom had the prime boarder back from the trail ride she had indeed taken. She was already busy currying and brushing the big black animal. "Thanks for helping, Jan," Mom said. "I got a little behind today."

"That's okay. Did the vet say when she's going to do the x-rays?"

"She'll come soon. Meanwhile, I'm going to start finishing off the shed."

"When?"

"After we eat."

"In the dark?"

"I can run a power cord out from the barn and rig up a light."

It occurred to Jan that except for Sundays, when her mother did nothing more than feed and water the boarders, she had no time for a major project like turning the shed into a closed room.

"I want to help you, Mom," Jan said. She said it firmly because Mom preferred doing jobs by herself. Her claim was she got them done faster that way. "Dad taught me how to hammer a nail in straight, you know."

Her mother gave one of her half smiles. "If you want, you could start clearing tack out of the barn. We can't put a horse in that room until every hook and nail he could hurt himself on is gone."

"Did you find another boarder?"

"Could be. We'll see." Mom wrinkled her forehead and said, "I wonder if Dr. Foster would let me pay her in installments." Thinking out loud, she added, "I hate to ask her, though. She hasn't been charging us as much as she should lately as is."

By "lately" Mom meant since Dad died. "Dr. Foster's nice," Jan said. "You're right. We should pay her up front."

"Okay. Tomorrow we'll go to the bank and take out your money."

And if the x-rays showed that Dove needed further treatment? Expensive treatment? No doubt Mom would bring up the leasing idea again. Just thinking about it made Jan shiver. So don't think, she told herself. Dad would say worrying was useless because nothing worked out the way you expected it to. Mom was the worrier in the family, the one who spotted black clouds in every blue sky. No wonder she had permanent frown lines on her forehead.

"I'm afraid it's another soup-and-sandwich night," Mom said. "I didn't have time to get to the grocery store, and we're out of most everything."

"Fine with me," Jan said. So long as something filled her stomach, she wasn't fussy. That was probably why, for all the long length of her, she didn't weigh a hundred and thirty pounds. "Slim," her father had called her affectionately. "If you weren't tall like me, you'd make a good jockey." But she was tall with long legs and an angular face that wasn't quite pretty. She would rather have been small and cute like Mattie.

46

At school Friday morning, Brittany invited Jan to a Halloween party at her house. "You've been in classes with most of the kids who're coming. And Lisa, the new girl, says she lives near you, so she can give you a ride if your mom can't bring you."

"Really? You asked someone to give me a ride, Brittany?" Jan was touched. She hadn't known Brittany liked her well enough to do that much for her.

"Yeah. So will you come?"

"Sure."

Now that Jan knew her lunch partner's name, she used it when greeting her in the hall. "Lisa? Brittany says you live near me. But we don't ride the same school bus, do we?"

It turned out that Lisa lived in a development of patio homes halfway between the ranch and the school but still several miles from the ranch. Nevertheless, Lisa assured Jan that her mother would be glad to pick her up and take her back after the party.

Jan rode the school bus home wondering if she'd be expected to wear a costume. No doubt, since it was a Halloween party. Well, she could always go in cowgirl getup. It felt good that Brittany had invited her and that Lisa was still being friendly. Could she invite them to the ranch to repay them? Brittany wasn't that interested in horses, but Lisa had owned a horse. Except Jan couldn't offer to let them ride because Dove wasn't well, and

Mom couldn't allow the boarders' horses to be ridden without their owners' permission.

Probably neither girl would be interested in coming to the ranch, anyway. And what could Jan feed them? When Mom did remember to stock their refrigerator, all she bought was processed cheese, bread, and fruit. Of course, she could ask Mom to get cookies and soda for a change. Their budget wasn't so tight they couldn't afford a bag of cookies. And if both Brittany and Lisa came, they could talk to each other so that Jan wouldn't get stuck making conversation. But the casita was awfully small. Jan tried to imagine entertaining two girls in a living room just big enough for two chairs, an end table, and a TV. Well, she'd see. Maybe she'd invite them. If she felt brave enough.

Mom was lungeing a horse in the arena when Jan got home. It was the gray big-headed animal that had started chewing up its stall in the barn. Mom had warned his owner that the horse was getting bored from lack of exercise, but the owner had a million excuses for not getting to the ranch to attend to his animal.

"He paying you for that?" Jan asked her mother, the "he" being the owner.

"No, but I couldn't let this old fool demolish any more of his gate. You should have seen how happy he was to get out. He just lay down and rolled in the dirt soon as he got in the ring." .

"Mom, I'm invited to a Halloween party."

"Oh? You going?"

"I'd like to."

"Well, good."

Mom didn't ask any further questions. She never had been one for the kind of safety quiz other mothers put their children through when they wanted to go somewhere. "What kind of mother are you, anyway?" Jan teased her. "Don't you want to know who's giving it and where it is and stuff like that?"

"Do I need to? I expect you know to behave yourself," Mom said. She gave Jan a quick glance, then turned back to lungeing the gray horse. "Dr. Foster stopped by. Said it was convenient to take the x-rays today because she had work to do out this way."

Jan tensed and grabbed the pipe railing for support. "She took them already? Did she find anything?"

Mom nodded. "Looks like Dove needs an operation."

Jan caught her breath. "A serious one?"

"Well, Dr. Foster said it'll *be* serious if he doesn't get one."

"What's he got?"

"A thing called constriction of the palmar annular ligament. It's kind of like carpal tunnel syndrome in people. Only it's in his right front leg."

"And is that kind of operation— Will it cost a fortune?"

Instead of answering, Mom said, "I guess we could leave this fellow out here in the arena to exercise himself for a while." She headed for their casita and Jan followed.

"Mom, how much?" Jan asked her mother's back.

"I called the bank and made an appointment about getting a loan," Mom said.

"You'd do that for Dove?"

"No. For you," Mom said.

Jan couldn't believe it. "But you hate owing money! And how will we pay it back? Oh, Mom, no! You're figuring we can lease Dove to pay off the loan, aren't you? But I can't. I just can't do that."

"Well, we'll see," her mother said calmly. "After the shed's done, maybe I could get a job nights."

"You can't work two jobs." The very idea of it was unfair. Jan sat down next to her mother on the bench on their ramada and leaned toward her. "You already get so tired you fall asleep in front of the TV after supper," she said.

"I used to waitress before I met your father," Mom said. "There's good money in that. Would you mind being out here alone nights?"

"I'd mind you working two jobs." Jan got tears in her eyes. "I mean, I appreciate that you're willing. I didn't think you— I mean, you didn't want Dad to get me a horse. And I guess you were right that we couldn't afford Dove. But now he's part of the family and—" Tears slid down Jan's cheeks. "I don't know what to say. I feel so bad, Mom." She was overwhelmed by guilt that her mother should have to do all the sacrificing to save a horse she'd never wanted in the first place.

"If Dove doesn't get the operation, Dr. Foster says he'll get worse," Mom said. "We'd have to have him put down, Jan."

Jan caught her breath. "No," she said. "Oh, no! But there must be another way to get the money."

"I haven't thought of any."

"What about Grandma?"

Mom snorted. "Last time I asked her for a loan was when your father died. She said then she had to think of her old age and that I'd best get rid of the ranch and find sensible work."

"So you sold our house."

"Right, and that's about all we can sell if I want to stay employed." Mom chewed her lip. "Listen, I can quit waitressing once we pay off the bills. It's not like I'm going to have to work two jobs forever."

"I wish I was old enough to get a job," Jan said fiercely.

"Well, you're not, so don't even think about it. If you still want to cash in your savings account, we'd better go to the bank."

"I'm ready," Jan said, "And when we're back, I'll feed and water the horses for you."

Mom reached out and touched her arm. "You're a good girl," she said. "I worried some that your father spoiled you, but I guess he didn't."

"Oh, Mom!" Jan threw her arms around her mother and burst out with all her pent-up grieving. "I miss him so much, and I know you do, too."

Hastily, Mom shook Jan off and stood up. "We'd better go now," she said. "I'll get the keys to the pickup."

Jan trembled as she worked at getting herself under control before her mother came back out of the casita. She should have known better than to get emotional about Dad. Mom could only deal with her grief by burying it. That was how she was. But, at least, Jan now knew that her mother's remoteness didn't mean she didn't love her.

Jan dragged the hose from stall to stall to refill water drums for the horses. She changed Dove's water last. Then she leaned her head against his neck, feeling it pulse as he drank. He splattered her with drops when he shook his head after he'd finished.

"You've got to have an operation, Dove," she told him. For once she was glad he didn't have human understanding. It was better for him not to know what was going to happen to him, but she wished she could talk to someone about the operation, someone who could understand how scary it was. Mattie! She loved horses. Was it too late to visit her? They'd be eating dinner soon in the main house.

Jan ran across the dirt road and through the field, slowing only as she approached the back door. She could see through the dining room windows, which didn't need shades to keep out the sun because they faced the mountains to the north. The tables were set for dinner, but nobody was seated yet. Timidly, Jan knocked at the door. She hoped it would be Mattie who answered, but it was the manager.

"Well, hi," Stella said. "Did you come to see Mattie?"

"I was hoping to, yes."

"She's not feeling too well. One of her bad days. She's lying down, but I'll tell her you're here."

"No, no. I don't want to bother her if she's sick." Jan hesitated. "She's not very sick, is she? I mean, she looks so healthy."

"Most of the time. But she has her spells, as she calls them. She was injured in a car accident five or six years ago, and she gets headaches and forgets things." Stella smiled at Jan and confided, "If you could come by next Friday, that'd be so nice. Next Friday's her birthday."

"It is?" Jan said in surprise. "Okay, I'll try." She began backing away. Next Friday evening was Brittany's party, but there would probably be time before it to see Mattie.

"I'll let her know you were here," Stella said. "She talks about you a lot, calls you her 'young friend.' She's real tickled that you pay attention to her."

"Well, I like her," Jan said.

"Oh, Mattie's a cutie. They don't come any sweeter. Next Friday's Halloween, you know. Don't forget to come," Stella said again.

Jan couldn't fall asleep that night. Her mind was a rock tumbler polishing worries about how Dove's operation would go and how Mom was going to work two jobs when she was already tired from one. And Mattie was having a birthday! It would be fun to give her something—flowers, maybe, or candy. How hard was it to make fudge? That would work as a birthday gift. Jan could even save some of it to offer Brittany and Lisa—if she ever got up the nerve to invite them over. But that would have to wait because she was going to be very busy. Dove would need lots of attention when he had his operation and while he was recovering. And Mom deserved any help Jan could give her around the ranch.

Finally, Jan couldn't lie still another minute. She tiptoed out of the bedroom so as not to wake her mother, who was snoring as usual. Above the refrigerator was an old, yellowed cookbook. *The Joy of Cooking.* Jan looked up fudge and decided it was doable. She wrote "baking chocolate" on the shopping list Mom kept on the refrigerator door.

If she was going to be awake all night, Jan thought she might as well go check out the stars. She turned her back on the city lights and looked up toward the mountains etched dark against a slate sky. Was Dad out there somewhere amongst all those shiny stars? Did he know about their problem with Dove? If he knew and couldn't help them, he'd feel bad. Probably being dead meant he couldn't feel anything anymore. At least, the minister had said that death brought eternal rest. And that was good. Because right now Dad would be feeling really bad for his family.

An owl hooted somewhere. Jan blinked and shivered in the chill of the desert night. The temperature had dropped thirty degrees since the sun went down. Her warm bed began to seem appealing. This time, when Jan put her head down on the pillow, sleep snatched her right away.

CHAPTER SIX

Saturdays were always busy days for Mom. Owners who worked all week arrived to ride their horses, complain, ask for favors, and give excuses for not paying their horse's boarding fee that month. The parking area was criss-crossed with cars and pickups, and the center aisle in the barn was jammed with people grooming their horses. Jan finished her usual chores and then worked steadily at stripping the tack room. What time she had left she spent with Dove.

Sunday, Mom worked on enclosing the shed, and Jan helped her measure and cut and nail boards in place.

Between school, homework, and helping her mother with chores, as well as taking care of Dove, Jan stayed very busy all week. On Thursday night, she made her fudge, stirring and testing, stirring and testing, until a drip from the end of a fork formed a soft ball in a glass of cold water.

When the candy cooled enough to cut, she tasted a corner piece that had crumbled at the edge. Lo and behold, it was good!

Feeling triumphant, Jan packed the fudge in plastic wrap in a small pink-and-white box that had once held stationery her grandmother had sent her. She pasted a square of white paper over the label on the box, and wrote, "Happy birthday, Mattie. Your friend, Jan." The remainder of the candy went into the freezer for any possible future entertaining.

Her plan was to scoot over and deliver the candy after school Friday before getting ready for Brittany's party. She *was* supposed to wear a costume, and early in the week Mom had offered her a matador outfit.

"I didn't know you'd saved it," Jan had said when Mom surprised her by pulling the elegant black braided jacket and tight knee pants out of a box under the bed.

Mom had shrugged. "Didn't your father tell you how I tried my hand at bullfighting?"

"But he made it sound like—" Jan didn't want to say "a joke," but Dad *had* made her laugh when he told the story.

"Like I wasn't serious about it?" Mom asked. "Well, I was. It was my big dream. When your father met me, I was practicing on the bulls on his father's ranch."

"Then why did you give up so easily?"

Mom shrugged. "Nothing easy about it, Jan. A bull

hung me up on his horns my first time in the ring. Your father sat by my bedside, persuading me to marry him while he fed me my meals. He kept saying I was better with horses than with fighting bulls. Considering all the bones I'd broken, I decided he had a point."

The matador pants barely covered Jan's knees, but she had a pair of white tights that spanned the gap between foot and knee, and she liked the way she looked in the short-waisted, broad-shouldered jacket. She tied her hair back and said, "I look just like a boy."

"No way. You've got girl written all over your face." The way Mom said that was as near as she had ever gotten to telling Jan she was pretty.

Friday afternoon, Jan was eager to get into the matador suit. She gave Dove a quick hello, got the box of fudge, and raced over to present it to Mattie, whom she hadn't seen all week. Amelia was sitting alone in the shade on the back patio.

"Hi," Jan said. "It's me. The girl with the horse you met the other day when you were walking with Mattie?"

"Oh, yes. I remember," the dignified woman said. Her head had been tilted toward the mountains. Now she turned it toward Jan. "They're there, aren't they?" she asked. "The mountains? I can't see them anymore, but I suspect they're still there."

"They're red right now because the sun's going down soon," Jan said.

"Yes, I remember." Amelia's slight smile barely lifted her lips.

"Is Mattie around?"

"Sulking in her room. Her daughter was supposed to take her out for lunch, so Mattie spent the whole morning boasting about how she was going out. And then the daughter came by and gave her some wilted daisies and left. Not a word about the lunch. My sons would never do that to me. They don't come often, but at least they come when they say they will."

"That sounds pretty mean," Jan said.

"Selfish is more like it. I suspect Mattie spoiled her daughter because she was an only child."

"I'm an only child," Jan said.

"Well, are you spoiled?"

"I don't think so. At least, not very."

"Good for your folks, then. They must have brought you up right."

"I'm going to go find Mattie," Jan said. She went inside. A woman with saggy cheeks and dyed brown hair that showed a couple of inches of white roots was reading the newspaper. She stared briefly at Jan without smiling or speaking. Jan nodded at her and glanced in the kitchen hoping to see Stella, but nobody was there. She went to Mattie's room—her own room less than a year ago, although that was hard to believe.

"Come in," Mattie said quietly when Jan knocked on the door.

"Happy birthday," Jan said, holding the box out as she stepped inside. There sat Mattie in a flowered dress with a pink silk scarf around her neck facing Stella, who was sitting on a footstool. The whites of Mattie's eyes were pink as if she'd been crying, and she was clutching a handkerchief.

"Well, look who's here!" she said, her voice rising with delight. "My young friend. How nice to see you."

"I came to wish you a happy birthday," Jan said. She thrust the box at Mattie again.

"My goodness! Can you believe it, Stella? Look! The child knows it's my birthday. And what's this?" She received the box with much care, as if it might hold precious cargo.

"Just some candy I made for you," Jan said. "I'm not much of a cook. I hope it's all right."

"Oh, I can't believe it!" Mattie said. "You made something for me? That's just the sweetest—" She hopped up and embarrassed Jan to no end by hugging her, especially since Mattie's head only came to the middle of Jan's chest. Jan grimaced at Stella, who was grinning from ear to ear.

"See," Stella said. "I told you everybody loves you, Mattie." Stella got up. "I'll leave you two and get back to work now."

While Mattie was fussily opening the box of candy, Stella walked past Jan and bent to whisper in her ear, "Thanks for coming, kiddo."

Nothing would do but Jan had to eat a piece of her

own candy with Mattie. Over and over, Mattie told her how delicious it was, repeating that she couldn't believe that Jan had made it for her. Jan didn't remember ever getting so much gratitude for anything she'd done.

"So how's your horse? What's his name again?"

"Dove," Jan said. "He's got to have an operation."

Mattie wanted the details and Jan told her all about it.

"Your mother's going to take out a loan from the bank?" Mattie said. "My, she must love you a whole lot to do that."

Jan nodded, reluctant to talk about the loan. It weighed on her conscience because she knew what a dreadful burden it would be on Mom. "You look pretty in that dress," Jan told Mattie truthfully.

"Do I, honey? Well, I got dolled up because— Well, I thought I was going somewhere special, but—" She shrugged. Absently, she rotated the ring on her hand. "My daughter gave me a birthday gift, too," she said finally. She indicated the droopy flowers in a vase on the green dresser. "Daisies are one of my favorites. She always remembers my birthday with something nice."

The dresser stood cheek by jowl with another made of heavy dark wood. The green dresser matched a green bed frame and chair that were obviously Mattie's side of the overstuffed room. Even without the occupants of the room being present, their furniture described the difference between the two women. Mattie's light green wood pieces were prettily decorated with flowers. Amelia's massive carved dresser and bed looked impressive and expensive.

"Do you like daisies, too?" Mattie asked.

"Uh-huh," Jan said, although she didn't admire that sad bouquet. "I like your ring," she offered in an attempt to change the subject.

Mattie's face lit up. She immediately held her hand out for Jan to see the square green stone surrounded by smaller stones. "My husband gave me this. It's a real emerald, and those are real diamonds around it. It cost way more than he could afford, but he said he had to give me something as special as I was. He always said sweet things like that. He was a loving man."

"Were you married a long time?"

"We were married twenty-five years before he died. I had twenty-five of the most happy years— That's lucky, isn't it? Not many people can claim a quarter of a century of wedded bliss. But now I've been a widow forty years. Imagine. I *can't* imagine it myself."

Jan was good at math. "So you're about eighty-five today, Mattie?"

She giggled. "That's right, eighty-five, but you better tell me I don't look it or I'll be mad at you."

"You don't look it," Jan said sincerely.

"Well," Mattie said. "When I brush my hair, I see all eighty-some years in the mirror, but, anyway, I'm glad to be alive still. And sure glad to see you. You made this the happiest birthday I've had in years, honey. I mean it, really."

Jan didn't know how to leave after that heartfelt statement. She asked if Mattie was going to have dinner soon, and Mattie said, "Not for a while. Want to go for a walk? I haven't been out today. I was waiting. Seems when I was young, I was always waiting for something to happen. I thought the waiting would stop when I grew up, but it never has." She smiled at Jan and said, "It's nice to walk in the evening. I never get tired of these Arizona sunsets, do you?"

"I'm sort of in a hurry tonight. I'm going to a party," Jan said, thinking uneasily that she still had a lot to do to get ready for it.

"Well, how about I walk you home? I'd just like to say hello to that sweet horse of yours. I won't stay but a minute."

Mattie was not to be denied. She swept through the living room, where five old ladies who were waiting for their dinners to be served were now staring at the TV screen. Gleefully, Mattie called out to them, "My young friend's going for a walk with me before supper. Be right back."

Amelia, who had come inside, looked up and shook her head as if she thought Mattie's enthusiasm was silly. Jan felt slightly foolish to have so much fuss made over her meager attentions, and she was impatient to get ready for the party now, but she couldn't hurt Mattie's feelings by telling her not to come.

Dove was standing in the middle of his corral. His ears hung low and the elegant head he always held so high was down beside his bad leg. "Oh, Dove, look at you," Jan said.

His dulled brown eyes met hers. Dove had become one unhappy horse.

"Oh, my!" Mattie said. "It's hard to see an animal suffer, especially a horse. It's a good thing he's going to have that operation. When will it be?"

"As soon as the bank gives Mom the loan, she'll call the vet and they'll schedule it," Jan said.

"Well, anything I can do, you let me know," Mattie said. "My goodness, you are something, thinking of me and my birthday when you've got trouble like this."

While Jan curried and brushed Dove, Mattie stayed, talking at him, and Dove seemed to cheer up listening to her chirp away. Just having Mattie there while she attended to Dove made Jan feel better, too. But the sun was sitting on the humps of the low mountains to the west, and in a few minutes it would be dark.

"I'd best get back," Mattie said.

"I'll go with you," Jan said.

"No, you don't have to. I'm pretty steady on my feet. Just when I have my spells I'm not so good. But I'm fine today."

Jan watched Mattie march back across the field. Halfway across she faltered, and tilted as if she might fall. Jan sprinted to catch up and took her arm.

"Nothing wrong. I just took a misstep, that's all," Mattie said. She didn't try to keep Jan when they got back to the house. "You go along now," she said. "And thanks for everything. You made my birthday something special."

Jan was wearing the matador outfit and wondering where her mother was when she heard the truck pull up outside. She put soup on to heat for another soup-and-sandwich supper. It was fortunate she'd set the burner on low. Otherwise, she might have let the soup boil over, because what her mother had to tell her blanked everything from her mind.

"The bank turned me down on the loan," Mom said. "They claim I don't have enough collateral left with what else I owe. I argued, but—" Mom's face was screwed up in pained apology.

Jan couldn't meet her mother's eyes. She said, "No loan? Then what about the operation?"

"I don't know, Jan. We'll try and think of something else."

But there wasn't anything else they could do. Jan stood frozen in a black panic. She was still lost in it when Lisa came to the door to pick her up for the party. Both Lisa and the party seemed remote now, beyond the range of Jan's emotions or understanding.

"You ready?" Lisa said. "Hey, I like your costume. You're a matador, right?"

Lisa had on a black dress with veils and spangles. "I'm a witch," she said when Jan just stood there without saying anything.

Lisa's frown of confusion activated Jan. "I can't go," she said abruptly. "Something went wrong and I just can't go. I'm sorry, Lisa. I'm sorry, but— Tell Brittany I'm sorry, too, will you?"

"What's the matter?" Lisa asked.

Jan opened her mouth and closed it again. Lisa had arranged for her mother go out of her way to pick Jan up. Jan owed her some explanation, but if she tried to tell the whole story, she'd break down and cry. "I just can't go," she said. "I'm really sorry." And she closed the door in Lisa's face.

CHAPTER SEVEN

Nothing felt good to Jan as she cleaned out stalls and fed and watered horses that Saturday after Halloween. A cold weight had settled in her chest. She tried and failed and tried again to think of a way to get the money for Dove's operation now that the bank wouldn't lend it.

At breakfast, Mom said, "There are loan places that advertise they'll give you money no matter what, but they charge such high interest that we'd never get the loan paid off. We'd likely end up losing the rest of the ranch and Dove in the bargain."

"Then let's not do that," Jan agreed soberly.

Sunday morning, after an hour of watching her mother worry her lower lip in silence, Jan suddenly realized that Mom wasn't coming up with a new idea. She was as stumped as Jan was. They were standing on either side of Dove, patting him down and loving him up, but he had retreated too deep into his suffering to be reached. Even his usually shiny coat was dull, and he couldn't seem to hold his head up for long. In desperation Jan said, "I'll call Grandma."

Mom shook her head. "She won't be willing to help for a horse. If you told her it was *you* who needed the operation, maybe."

"I can't lie, Mom. Can I?"

"No, I expect not. Well, now's a good time to try her. Should be evening in London. Maybe she'll do it for you, seeing as you're her one and only granddaughter."

Jan hated calling her grandmother in the best of circumstances. That imperious lady spoke in such an accusing way that right after "Hello" she could make Jan feel guilty. When Dad was alive, he'd called his mother dutifully, but he'd spent as little time in her presence as possible. "She hated ranch life, didn't think much of my dad or me, either," he'd said once. Jan had no doubt Grandma felt the same way about her and her mother.

She punched in the little-used overseas telephone number and perched on a kitchen chair, gripping the receiver while the phone rang.

"Yes?" Grandma's voice answered on the third ring.

"This is Jan. How are you, Grandma?"

"Jan? Is that you?"

"Yes, it's me." And because she couldn't think of any other small talk, she repeated, "How are you?"

"Not too well, if you really want to know. It's hard to get

up in the morning, and I can't find a way to lie in bed that doesn't pain me. What are you calling about?"

Jan swallowed and persisted in being polite. "I'm sorry you aren't feeling well. How's your husband—I mean, Grandpa?" She disliked using the term for a man she barely knew, but it was what her grandmother had asked her to call her new husband.

"No worse, no better."

"That's too bad," Jan said inadequately.

"Yes, it is," Grandma said. "And how's school? You're not in trouble, are you?"

"No. I'm fine. And so is Mom. I'm passing my courses okay. But . . . It's my horse."

"Horse?" Grandma snorted. "It would be a horse. That's all you people out there care about. Well, what's the problem with your horse?"

"This is Dove, the horse Dad gave me? He's got a bad leg and he needs an operation."

"How unfortunate. I suppose that means money."

"Yes. Mom asked the bank, but they won't lend it to her."

"And no doubt you've already spent what I sent you for your birthday and Christmas."

"No, Grandma. But I had to pay for the x-rays, and that took all I had."

Grandma made a sound of disgust. Then she said what she'd said many times before. "It's time you and your mother realized that horses are for rich people. You can't afford to live on a ranch. She can't make a living trying to run one. Even your father couldn't make a profit from that dry-bones little place. And now you're in trouble and you expect me to bail you out?"

"I need a thousand dollars, maybe more," Jan admitted.

She wasn't surprised when her grandmother answered promptly. "Don't expect to get it from me. I haven't got money to waste. And fixing up that animal just means something else will happen to it to cause more expense. Sorry." But she didn't sound sorry.

"I hope you feel better soon, Grandma," Jan said quietly. And she hung up.

When her mother asked her if she'd made the phone call, Jan nodded. "You were right. She wouldn't lend us anything—not for a horse." And probably not for us, either, Jan thought privately.

On Monday in school, Jan found Brittany talking animatedly to a group of kids perched on desks around her. Timidly, Jan tapped Brittany on the shoulder and said, "I'm sorry I didn't get to your party Friday. I really wanted to come. But something happened with my horse, and I just had to deal with it."

The minute Brittany looked up at her, Jan could see by the coldness in her eyes that any liking Brittany had had for her was gone. "Well, you missed a good party," Brittany said. She paused and added with disdainful emphasis, "because of your horse." Then she turned her back on Jan and leaned toward her group. "Wasn't that hysterical when Mark's wig dropped in the punch?"

The others laughed with her.

Jan backed away. It hurt to have lost the one friend she'd had in school. Although there was still Lisa. But Lisa wasn't in homeroom, and Jan didn't know where she might be. If she could just find Lisa and explain what had happened, it might put things right again between them. Last Friday night, Jan had been too upset to explain anything.

Lisa walked in after first-period class had started and handed the teacher an excuse slip about a dentist appointment.

"I need to talk to you," Jan said to her in the hall during change of class.

"I don't have time now," Lisa said.

At lunchtime, Jan got in line behind Lisa to buy milk and an apple. Lisa turned and said accusingly, "My mother was mad at me for making her drive so far out of the way to pick you up—and then you didn't come. What's wrong with you? Is it me you don't like? Or are you just antisocial?"

"I couldn't—I just couldn't go to a party that night, Lisa. I'm sorry. It wasn't you. I mean, you've been very nice to me, and—" Jan swallowed and got stuck in the knot of excuses.

"Then why didn't you call or something?" Lisa asked. "You made me get yelled at. My mom hates driving at night. I only offered because I thought— Well, you live near me and nobody much else does. But I guess you don't need friends."

Jan caught her breath. "Yes, I do," she said, but not soon enough for Lisa to hear her. She had handed the cashier her money and bounced off toward Brittany's table.

Jan ate alone at a table in the far corner of the cafeteria. She felt like a pariah. Well, she deserved to be. If only she had her father's skill with people! He would have sweet-talked Lisa out of her anger. Of course, Dad wouldn't have closed the door in Lisa's face Friday night, either. He had been graceful in social situations. He wouldn't have tromped all over people's feelings the way his daughter did.

That night again Jan couldn't sleep. She pulled on her boots over her bare feet, to protect against any scorpions still aboveground now that the summer's heat had gone, and went out to the barn. The air was thick with the ripe smell of manure and hay and warm horseflesh. Jan breathed deeply, straining to hear in the stillness the sounds of animals muttering and sighing in their sleep. Few things made her feel more peaceful than a barn full of horses at night.

She walked out the door and there was Dove lying under the shed roof at the barn end of his pipe corral. She slipped between the bars and went to him. Normally, he'd get up to greet her as soon as he sensed her presence. Tonight he just lay on his side with his hurt leg stuck at an awkward angle across his other front leg. She touched his head, afraid that he might not be breathing, but his eyelashes tickled the edge of her palm as he blinked.

"Dove," she said, "Dove, what am I going to do? There's got to be a way to get money for you, if only I could think of it. Too bad you don't have a rich owner. If you were our prime boarder, you'd get that operation." She thought of Mom's leasing idea. Hateful as it might be to share Dove, it *was* a way to bring in money. Tell Mom she'd relented? But even so, they couldn't lease Dove until he was well. First they had to borrow the money for the operation. And who would lend them money if the bank and Grandma wouldn't?

Jan laid her head against Dove's smooth, warm neck and let the tears leak hotly onto him. He took a deep breath and let it out in a shuddering sigh. She closed her eyes wearily and dozed and woke and finally returned to bed.

Mattie and Amelia came walking down the road the next afternoon. With Mattie leading the way, they swerved and came straight to Dove's corral.

"How're you doing?" Mattie asked Jan, who was raking up the soiled shavings. It was a task she should have done that morning. But she'd awakened shivering and headachy, and by the time she'd taken a hot shower and pushed herself through the motions of dressing, she'd barely made the school bus. Then she'd endured another long school day of being one alone among many.

"Not so good," Jan said. She greeted Amelia with a "Hi," and got a wave of the hand in reply.

"When's the operation?" Mattie asked.

"No money. No operation," Jan said. "The bank refused Mom."

"Oh, honey, that's terrible. What are you going to do?"

"I don't know. Kill myself, maybe." Jan spoke without smiling.

"Now, that's no way to sound. There's always something you can do," Mattie said.

Amelia snorted. "When there's no money, there's no money. You should understand that. You gave all yours to your daughter, and now you're stuck rooming with me. Can't even have your own room because she won't pay for it."

"Oh, what do I need my own room for?"

"Because you want it bad. Admit it, Mattie, you know you want it."

"Well, there are other things more important. Besides, what'd you do without me?"

"I'd get along," Amelia said.

"Anyway, I didn't give my daughter everything," Mattie said. "I still have my emerald ring."

"Right, and she's probably aiming to get that away from you as soon as you land in the nursing home or you give her some other excuse to call you incompetent."

"My daughter's not nasty like you make her out to be,"

Mattie said angrily. "She's a good girl, and she and I have always been that close." She held up her crossed fingers to show Amelia. "It's just—I don't know. She's scared because I forgot to turn off the stove and like that. That's all it is."

"You mean she only loves you when you're useful to her?"

Mattie was bristly with distress. "Valerie's busy," she told Amelia. "She's got a high-up position in her company." Mattie stopped and looked startled as if she'd remembered something. Her eyes focused vaguely on Jan, who was stroking Dove's neck as she listened. Once again, Mattie had forgotten that her daughter had quit that job and was working as a consultant now, Jan thought.

But Mattie had hit her stride again. "And anyway, Amelia," she boasted, "the ring is still mine, and it's valuable. So I'm not poor."

"A lot of good that ring does you," Amelia said. "I put all my jewelry in the safe deposit box. Nothing to wear it for around here."

"I'll tell you what this ring'd be good for. It'd be good for a loan if I hocked it," Mattie said.

"Oh, pshaw!" Amelia said. "As if you need money."

"Well, I don't, but my young friend here does." She turned to Jan and said earnestly, "That's what we could do. We could hock this ring to get the money you need for the operation."

Jan's heart leaped at this spark of an idea and sank in the next instant as Amelia put it down.

"Are you crazy, Mattie?" Amelia said. "If you pawn that ring, where are you going to get the money to redeem it?"

"Don't you think this child and her mother would pay me back? Of course they would. You don't trust anybody, Amelia, but I do." She drew herself up tall as she could and narrowed her eyes as she considered. "Now," Mattie said, "likely they won't give full value, so I won't get as much as the ring's worth. But I bet it would cover the operation." She frowned determinedly.

Amelia said, "You're an old fool, Mattie. I don't blame your daughter for taking your money away from you."

"I couldn't take your money," Jan put in. But neither woman seemed to hear her.

Still directing her remarks at Amelia, Mattie said, "The ring's mine, and if that's what I want to do with it, who's to stop me?"

If only Mattie were her grandmother, Jan thought wistfully.

"Your daughter'll be sure you're crazy if she finds out you pawned it," Amelia warned.

Mattie paused to think, her eyes wide and her lips pursed with concentration. Finally, she said, "What if she doesn't find out? What if I say I lost it again?"

"Last time when you thought you lost it, she sounded ready to send you to the nursing home for being senile."

"She was just upset. She loves this ring, and it'll be hers

for sure when I die. Meanwhile, I don't see why it can't be of use to someone else."

"Mattie!" Jan raised her voice and touched Mattie's shoulder to make her listen. "I couldn't take your ring."

"Oh, no? What else are you going to do?" Mattie asked feistily.

Jan chewed on her lip in silence. She had no answer to that. She only knew it would be wrong to let Mattie pawn her ring. That wasn't a solution to consider. Resolutely, Jan put it out of her mind even while she said, "I guess I'll think of something." Her remark was sheer bravado. She knew her brain was squeezed dry of ideas.

CHAPTER EIGHT

When Jan went to take care of Dove before school Friday morning, he didn't bother to greet her. He didn't even show an interest in her presence. Worse, when she tried to coax him to get up so she could brush and curry him, he wouldn't budge.

"I know what'll get you up, Dove," she said. She raced to the casita, grabbed a slice of bread, and ran back to hold it out to him. Years before, when he'd nipped a sandwich right out of her hand, she had discovered how much he liked bread. Now he stretched his neck toward the treat without moving his legs. When he couldn't reach it, he pulled his lips back over his teeth in that horse smile that always made her smile back.

"Oh, Dove," she said, her voice choking with feeling, "you just have to move around more." She could hear Dad's voice warning of respiration problems if she let him lie there for too long. "Come on. Stand up, or I'm not giving this to you."

Finally, he heaved himself upright and took the bread. But

he rested all his weight on his three good legs while she groomed him.

"Things are bad enough without you developing any more ailments," she told him.

He bumped her shoulder playfully when she'd finished. "You know, we still haven't figured out how we're going to afford to get your leg fixed," she said. "But we will. Don't you worry, we will."

Maybe his leg would start healing by itself, she thought. After all, minor miracles did happen. Why not to Dove and her?

A pink sunrise lingered in the east and the air was still a chilly fifty degrees when she'd finished watering and feeding Dove. Jan just had time to use the bathroom before leaving for school. While she was sitting on the toilet, she saw evidence that her mother had taken to wishful thinking, too. In the wastebasket under the sink was a ripped-up lottery ticket. Mom never bet, but now she'd put good money down on a long shot, and Jan had no doubt for whom she'd done it. Mom, who had always been the realist in their family! Jan got tears in her eyes at this new sign of her mother's affection for her.

In gym that day, the teacher made the whole class run the mile for the quarterly fitness tests, and Jan ran the fastest.

Lisa appeared at her side in the hall on the way to lunch. "Did you get so strong from riding your horse?" Lisa asked.

"More likely from ranch work," Jan said, thinking that

even if riding could strengthen her, it wouldn't have, because she hadn't done any for weeks.

"Aren't you too young to be 'working'?" Lisa asked.

"Why? My mother needs help on the ranch. And I like doing it."

"I guess that makes sense," Lisa said. Then, with a sympathy that hadn't been in her voice before, she asked, "Is your horse any better?"

"No."

"Well, I'm sorry. I guess I don't know a lot about horses. Maybe you could introduce me to yours sometime? I mean, I'd be interested. Back East, we didn't have real ranches. Not where I lived in Connecticut, anyway."

"Okay, sure," Jan said quickly. She was delighted that Lisa was still offering her friendship even after all Jan's inept rebuffs, but only after Lisa had turned off into the girls' bathroom did Jan think about setting a date. "What's the matter with me?" she asked herself out loud. "Can't I even ask someone to come over?" Lisa had made it clear enough she wanted to come. Tomorrow, Jan told herself. Tomorrow she'd practice the fine art of making friends.

That afternoon after school, Jan found her mother in the big arena exercising a spirited paint on a lunge line. The paint was a young, partly schooled animal that belonged to a ten-year-old girl whose doctor mother couldn't always drive her to the ranch to work with him. Jan let herself in the gate and greeted Mom quietly so as not to upset the high-stepping black-and-white horse.

"You have a good day?" Mom asked.

"Okay. How's Dove doing?"

"I called Dr. Foster and asked if we could have the operation and pay her off in installments. She said *she'd* be willing, but she'd need to use the surgery facilities. That's where the major cost is. And she has no control over those charges. She sounded like she felt bad about not being able to help us out." Mom threw Jan a worried glance.

Jan pressed her thumb to her lip, thinking. Desperation made her say, "Mattie made an offer the other day. Did I tell you she has this ring her husband gave her that's worth a lot of money?"

Mom shrugged. She was concentrating on keeping pace with the frisky horse, who was kicking up his heels and tossing his head as he moved. Besides, she had no interest in jewelry. The only thing Mom ever wore was her thin gold wedding band.

"Well, Mattie said she could hock her ring and lend me the money for Dove," Jan continued.

"Do you think she meant it?"

"I don't know. Probably." Jan was recalling the feisty way Mattie had insisted on her right to do what she wanted with her own property. It had sounded as if she wanted to prove that she wasn't totally under her daughter's control.

"Well, even if she wasn't just talking," Mom said, "you

couldn't let her do it, Jan. She's an old lady and she may not be—you know, all there. It would be wrong to take her money."

"I know."

"Anyway," Mom said, "she's probably already forgotten she said it."

"Maybe," Jan said. But she wondered. Did having spells and forgetting things occasionally mean that Mattie had lost her mind? It seemed to Jan that Mattie made too much sense to be senile. Still, her spur-of-the-moment offer might not have been serious. Or she might have been boasting out of a passing anger at her daughter, and thought better of it later. In any case, they couldn't take her money when Mattie had so little herself—nothing but the ring, not even her own room.

"I bought another lottery ticket today," Mom said.

"You're wasting money, Mom."

"Somebody's got to get lucky. Why not us?"

"I guess," Jan said. A lottery ticket was a long shot, but it was better than nothing.

Mom slowed the paint to a standstill and began stroking his neck. "Imagine . . . your Mattie offering to hock her ring for you," Mom said. "That lady sure must like you a lot. Even if she didn't mean it, it was nice of her."

"Mattie is really nice," Jan said.

"One of these days I'd like to meet her." A smile creased Mom's sun-worn face. "Tell you what. How about we invite her for a cookout?"

82

"A cookout?" They never entertained. Jan wasn't even sure what her mother meant.

"Sure," Mom said cheerfully. "It'll get our minds off our troubles. I'll buy a steak and we can cook it outdoors. We still have that old charcoal grill of your father's. It doesn't have to be fancy. Mattie'd probably be glad to be invited out."

Jan was sure she would be, especially since her daughter didn't take her anywhere. "That'd be wonderful, Mom. But I think hamburger would be better than steak. I mean, in case she has false teeth or something."

"Right," Mom laughed. "Hamburger and buns and some salad is enough. Want to invite her for tomorrow?"

"Tomorrow's Saturday."

"So?"

"It's your busiest day," Jan said.

"You can help me get the horses done early, and we've got to eat, anyhow. How about it?"

Jan smiled. "Sounds good to me. I'll go invite her right now."

"Be sure you say that it's only going to be a light supper. I don't want her expecting a gourmet feast."

"Don't worry. I'll tell her you can't cook."

"Who says I can't cook?" Mom yelled, but Jan just laughed as she ran off toward the big house. It felt good to be doing something sociable for a change.

Stella greeted her at the back patio door. When Jan said

83

she'd come to see Mattie, Stella said, "Mattie's taking a nap. I'm just about to go home for the weekend, but I could leave her a message for you."

"Well, my mother and I want to invite her for supper tomorrow night."

Stella clapped her hands in delight, as if the invitation were for her. "Terrific! Mattie'll be in seventh heaven to be invited out. She loves to party. I'll tell the woman who works here weekends to see to it she's ready at . . . ?"

"Five o'clock?"

"Perfect. You'll come to pick her up, won't you?"

"Sure," Jan said.

"I wish I could see her face when she gets the invitation. She'll be so thrilled," Stella said.

Jan walked away from the house smiling at how pleased Stella had been for Mattie's sake. Mattie's daughter might not care about her as much as she should, but other people in her life did.

CHAPTER NINE

Cleaning the house and making a salad in preparation for
Mattie's visit distracted Jan from brooding about Dove on
Saturday. That morning she had found him lying down
again. Mom had wrapped his leg to try and give him some
relief, and he had finally risen and hobbled to his feeder to
eat.

"Looks like he hasn't lost his appetite, anyway," Mom
said. She patted Dove on his rump and went back to work.
Jan had waited patiently for him to finish chewing his hay
and drinking. Then she'd tried walking him around his corral on a lead line. She was still going by her father's belief
that a horse needed exercise no matter what. But Dove followed her reluctantly.

It pained her to see him limping, this horse who had
been so playful that he'd toss lengths of rope and chase them
all by himself. He'd watch what was going on around the

barn and follow anyone walking past his corral as far as he could. Dove had only lain down voluntarily to sleep at night.

"Come on. You'll feel better if you exercise," Jan coaxed as she tugged at the lead line.

He didn't seem to feel better, though. He hobbled along with his head hanging, and when she gave up after a few yards of tugging at him, he sighed with relief. Was he getting worse? Jan asked herself anxiously. Without the operation, how long would it be until he couldn't stand up and move at all? Dove gave a pathetic groan and settled back down on the ground. The sound cracked open Jan's heart.

By a quarter of five, every horse had been fed and watered. Jan told her mother, who was washing up at the kitchen sink in their casita, that she was going to pick up Mattie.

"I'll start the fire in the grill," Mom said. "I bought a fresh bag of charcoal in case that stuff of your father's is too old to burn."

Jan nodded. She hoped Mattie wouldn't be disappointed with hamburgers and beans, plus the tub of macaroni salad and brownies her mother had bought at the deli. "Thanks for doing this, Mom," Jan said.

"Haven't entertained since your father died," Mom said. "Not that I was much good at it before. But he was always bringing home people he liked."

"I know," Jan said. Those unexpected social occasions had been fun. Dad had not only made the fires but also kept up lively conversations with the guests. She and Mom needed only to be stagehands for his performance. Jan wished he were here to run the show tonight.

"We used to keep beer in the refrigerator for guests," Mom said anxiously. "I hope Mattie won't expect any. I didn't think of buying alcoholic beverages when I was shopping."

"I'm sure she'll be too polite to ask, Mom. Don't worry. Mattie's easy."

And she was. When Jan was ushered into the living room of the big house by a white-uniformed woman she'd never met, Mattie was there, sitting on the couch. She was decked out in a blue silk dress with red buttons and a red belt, so intent on chatting away at two other old ladies that she didn't notice Jan had come.

"I'm Jo. I'm here weekends," the heavyset middle-aged woman told Jan. "Mattie's been twittering all over the place about going out with you."

Mattie looked over her shoulder then and spotted Jan. She bobbed to her feet, caroling, "Here's my young friend! My date's come, everybody. You all have a good dinner, now. See you later." Smiling, Mattie waved at the silent assembly of women and took Jan's arm, as if she really were going off on an important date.

Once they were outside, Mattie said, "Imagine you inviting me to your house! It's just so nice. And I have a surprise for you."

For the first time, Jan noticed Mattie was carrying a thin rectangular box that didn't look as if it could hold more than a scarf or a pair of gloves or, most useless of all, a handkerchief. It was gift-wrapped and tied with a red bow.

"Don't frown, now," Mattie said. She patted Jan's arm. "You're going to like this present."

"Mattie, you don't need to bring us anything," Jan protested. "It's not that much of a meal. Mom just wants to meet you."

"Well, I'm looking forward to meeting her. Believe you me, I am. Imagine!"

Mattie's excitement made Jan anxious. No way could she and her mother measure up to such a high level of expectation. As they walked toward the casita, Jan worried that the invitation had been a mistake.

"Your horse any better, honey?" Mattie asked. Her hand trembled lightly on Jan's arm.

"Uh-uh. Dove's miserable. He keeps lying down and it's hard to make him get up and move."

"Oh, my! Lying down's no good for horse or human. It makes your muscles weak. That's why I try to walk every day. It's important to stay healthy." Mattie nodded in agreement with herself. "Well, we're going to get help for that poor animal soon. Don't you worry." More quick birdlike taps on Jan's arm followed.

Mattie greeted Jan's mother with a hug, as if they were old friends, never mind that they'd never met. "I just know you're a lovely person because you're the mother of this sweet child. Did you know she made me a birthday present?"

Mom laughed. "I hope you didn't get sick from eating it. Jan and I aren't much for cooking. And you'd better be satisfied with hamburgers, because that's what we've got for supper."

"Oh, I love hamburgers. They're my favorite."

Mattie then went on to exclaim about how cute the casita was. "Just the right size for two women, isn't it?" she said.

Jan and her mother glanced at each other. "Actually, it's a pretty tight squeeze," Mom said honestly.

But Mattie wasn't listening. She was admiring the framed photographs on the wall behind the television: Mom on a bucking bronco in a rodeo, Dad with the first yearling they'd raised on their ranch, Jan sitting on top of Dove when she was seven and barely visible under her father's hat.

"Why, that hat almost fits you, doesn't it?" Mattie said with a sly grin.

The supper was a gourmet delight if Mattie was to be believed. Jan hadn't heard her mother laugh so much since Dad had died. Mattie was full of stories about her horse experiences and how her husband had spoiled her. All she said about her daughter was that Valerie had never taken to horses much and that she'd always been good in school.

"Don't know where she got it from," Mattie said. "I was never much of a student. Maybe my husband would have been if he'd had a chance, but he had to go to work so young. He came from a poor farm family. Though you'd never know it to speak to him. He was a real old-fashioned gentleman, just like my daddy. In fact, those two got along real well."

She described with some pride the property her own family had owned in Mississippi. "Until my daddy lost it all. He was a gambler, you know. A good man, but he did like to gamble."

The stars were out when Mattie looked at the clock and exclaimed, "I can't believe how the time has gone. It's my bedtime, and here I am, still out partying. Oh, my!" She turned to Jan. "You don't want to walk me home in the dark, honey. I'll just take off by myself and leave you to help your mama with the dishes."

"Jan will walk you," Mom said.

"Do you think she should be out alone this late?" Mattie asked anxiously.

"It's just on the ranch, after all. Like walking around your own property," Mom said.

"Well, I guess if you look at it that way, I'd be glad of an escort," Mattie said. "My eyes aren't good in the dark anymore. Thank you for this wonderful evening. I had such a lovely time. It's the most fun I've had in—oh, I can't tell you when."

She rose and Jan got up to take her arm. Then Mattie said, "I almost forgot. I have something here for you." She smiled and put the thin rectangular box, which she'd set down on the TV set, into Jan's hand.

"Now, don't be that way, honey," she said when Jan pulled back and shook her head. "You'll like this present. I know you will."

There was no polite way to get out of accepting it. "Thanks," Jan said. She took the box, but set it back down on the TV unopened. Getting presents embarrassed her, and she'd never been good at pretending to like something if she didn't. Better to open it in private and wear it once for Mattie to see, and thank her then. That was assuming the box held something wearable and not a photograph or something like that.

"Well," Mattie said, "I guess I'd better get on back to the house, hadn't I?" She seemed anxious to leave now, but not so anxious that she didn't spend five minutes thanking Mom again for the delicious meal and saying she just wished she could return the invitation, but she wasn't living in her own house anymore.

"I used to make the tastiest beef burgundy, so good you wouldn't believe it. But I don't even have my own room now, let alone a kitchen," Mattie said. She looked around. "This place may be small, but at least it's your own."

She was quiet on the walk back. "Are you all right?" Jan asked her when they got to the big house.

"Just a little tired, honey. You open that box when you get home, now. Hear? And let me know what you think about what's inside it."

"Okay, I'll tell you," Jan said. And on impulse she bent and kissed Mattie's cheek.

The echoes of Mattie's repeated good-byes followed her most of the way back to the casita.

"So," Jan said to her mother, "our first party was a big success, Mom. Maybe we should entertain more."

"Maybe," Mom said. She had washed up the few dishes by herself. "You'd better open that box so you can thank your friend for whatever she gave you."

"It's probably just something she had around," Jan said. "Something that I can't use. I mean, she doesn't get out to the mall or anyplace."

Carelessly, Jan ripped off the ribbon and the tissue-paper wrap and opened the box. Inside was a plastic Baggie. And inside the Baggie were hundred-dollar bills—fifteen hundred-dollar bills—enough money for Dove's operation.

"Oh, my!" Jan said in unconscious imitation of Mattie. "What do I do now?" She held out the box with the bills spread so her mother could see.

Mom looked stunned. "I don't know," she said. "So much money! It's unbelievable that she should— How do you think she got so much money?"

Jan didn't have to think very long. "Did you notice, was she wearing a ring?"

"I don't notice things like that."

"Me, neither, but she must have hocked her emerald ring somehow," Jan said.

"I hope not," Mom said. "Anyway, tomorrow we'd better go talk to that house manager and ask her what to do about this."

"I think Stella's only there during the week. Someone else was in charge tonight."

"Then we'll wait until Monday," Mom said. "Put that money out of your mind, Jan. My guess is we won't be able to keep it."

Despite her mother's warning, Jan couldn't stop thinking about the fifteen hundred dollars. She longed to rush over and thank Mattie for it, but how could she when she didn't know whether she was returning it or not? It made her squirm to think that the money would save Dove if it somehow turned out to be all right for her to keep it. There it was—happiness just within her grasp. But keeping the money did seem wrong, wrong because Mattie was weak and defenseless and maybe not as much in charge of her own possessions as she imagined. Wrong . . . and yet so tempting.

CHAPTER TEN

Until she knew what to do about the money—whether she had to thank Mattie and return it, or could thank Mattie and keep it—Jan wanted to avoid her benefactor. So Sunday she hid out in the barn. She oiled tack and groomed whatever horses needed more attention than they got from their owners. She patched Dove's horse blanket as best she could and devoted more time than usual to homework. Meanwhile, she was imagining how ungrateful Mattie must think she was since she hadn't yet thanked her.

Whenever Jan tried talking about it to her mother, Mom changed the subject. Finally, her mother said, "I can't see how you can rightly take that money, and I don't want you trying to persuade me that it's okay."

"But, Mom, as long as we repay Mattie, what's wrong with letting her help? You're willing to take on two jobs—" She paused briefly. "And I'm willing to lease Dove out. But

I want to pick the one who gets him, and we have to wait until he's well, of course."

"You're willing to lease him out now?"

Jan shuddered. "Well, I'm not glad about it, but I know it's necessary."

Mom nodded. "It's nice to know you've got some common sense in you," she said.

"So is it okay about borrowing from Mattie?"

Mom shook her head. "I don't want to discuss it," she said and walked away.

Jan let Mom be then. But she couldn't help thinking that anything they could do to save Dove should be acceptable. Mom was just leery of being beholden to anybody for anything. But this was an emergency, reason enough to make an exception. Dad would have known how to put it to Mom. He'd probably have been able to convince her that they were doing Mattie a favor by letting her lend them the money. No doubt it would make Mattie feel good. If only Jan had his persuasive powers! But at least Mom was willing to consult with Stella. That meant she *might* change her mind.

The more impatient Jan got for the school day to end on Monday, the more endless it seemed. Mom had promised to call and ask to see Stella that afternoon. Meanwhile, Jan fretted about how hurt Mattie must be that Jan hadn't said a word about her extraordinary gift.

In social studies they were starting on projects. Each group was to do a report and an oral presentation on one of the key countries listed on the chalkboard. Jan hated oral reports. She considered them a form of torture. Groups were forming around the classroom, but she didn't see any that was likely to welcome her enthusiastically. Why should they? Her research talent was only slightly better than her ability to make speeches. Her eyes met Lisa's. Lisa didn't have a group she could take refuge in, either.

"Want to work with me?" Jan asked her.

"Okay." Lisa nodded. "But just the two of us?" She glanced apprehensively at the list: Japan, Mexico, Russia, Canada, China.

"I guess they're kind of big topics, huh?" Jan said.

"Unless you want to do Mexico," Lisa suggested. "My family's traveled there, so I have a zillion slides. We could do like a travelogue."

Jan heaved a sigh of relief. "Fine. How about I run the projector and you do the talking?"

"Sure," Lisa agreed easily. "Let's ask Mr. Coss if he'll let us."

Another group was already doing Mexico, but their amiable social studies teacher poked his glasses farther up his pudgy nose and suggested to that group that they include Jan and Lisa. "These girls have slides. They could do an introductory overview to your presentation," he said.

"Yeah, sure." Carlos, who was always the leader in any

group, spoke for the other members and waved Jan and Lisa over. "The more we got, the better the grade, right, Mr. Coss?"

"Nice try, Carlos," Mr. Coss said as he turned away.

At lunchtime, Lisa fell in beside Jan and asked, "Want to talk about our presentation while we eat?"

"Sure. Let's do that," Jan said.

"So how's your horse?"

"Bad, but there's a chance we can borrow the money for the operation he needs."

"But you don't want to talk about it, right?" Lisa said.

"Well," Jan said. "It's a long story."

Lisa turned out to be a good listener. It took Jan five minutes to explain about the loan and how Mom felt about it. "If I'm lucky and Stella doesn't think it's wrong to take the money," Jan concluded, "Mom might give in."

"I'll keep my fingers crossed for you," Lisa said.

Jan took a deep breath and, to her own surprise, blurted out, "You wouldn't want to lease a horse, would you?"

"Huh? What do you mean, 'lease a horse'?" Lisa said.

"Well, it's like to go shares in him. We'd both ride him and take care of him. I mean, after Dove gets well—*if* we can borrow the money for the operation and *if* he gets well, that is. Then I'll need to find someone I trust to lease him so we can pay back the loan."

"And you'd trust me?" Lisa said.

97

Jan looked her in the eye and nodded.

Lisa's smile was radiant. "I don't know," she said. "But I'll ask my folks. How much would it cost? I mean, to lease him."

"I don't know. If your folks say yes, they could ask my mother."

"It would be fun to share your horse," Lisa said enthusiastically.

Jan smiled to cover her dismay. She still didn't like the idea.

They ate their lunches in silence then. To restart the conversation, Jan asked Lisa about her travels in Mexico. Lisa launched into a long-winded tale of mishaps with a car that kept breaking down en route to the next town, and Jan relaxed listening to her.

"Do you have any brothers or sisters?" Lisa asked when she'd finished.

"No," Jan said.

"Lucky you," Lisa said with so much passion it made Jan laugh. "I hate my little brother."

"Why?"

"Because his favorite fun thing is to make my life miserable."

"What does he do to you?"

"Rotten stuff. Like last night he signed his name on every sheet of my good stationery. And like he's scribbled all over the new wallpaper in my bedroom."

"That *does* sound rotten," Jan said, but she couldn't help smiling.

98

"You may not think so, but I'd trade your horse for my brother anytime," Lisa said. With that, her anger burst and drained, and they both laughed at the outrageousness of such an exchange.

On the other side of the cafeteria, Brittany's overcrowded table had begun shooting straws at each other. A cafeteria aide went to settle them down. "How come you're not sitting with Brittany?" Jan asked her newfound friend.

"Oh, you know, I'm quiet. I like to talk to one person at a time and sort of get to know them. You're quiet, too, like me."

"Yes," Jan said. The things she and Lisa had in common were beginning to wrap cozily around her. "So when are you going to come and see what living on a ranch is like?"

"Whenever you invite me."

"I want to, but first I've got to find out what's going to happen with Mattie's loan," Jan said.

"I understand," Lisa said. And by the serious look in her eyes, Jan guessed she did.

When she got home from school that afternoon, Jan found Mom in the barn shaving a bridle path on top of a horse's head to allow the halter to lie flat over his mane.

"Did you call Stella?" Jan asked.

Mom looked up at her and said, "She says she'll stop by the casita after she finishes work and the evening woman comes on duty."

"Is she bringing Mattie?"

"No, I thought it'd be best if we just talked it over with her first."

"You'll do the talking?" Jan asked.

"No. You will. Just tell her what Mattie did and we'll see how it hits her."

Jan went to spend the waiting time with Dove. "Now what?" she asked him when she saw that he still had half the hay she had left for him that morning. "If you're off your feed, you must really be in a bad way."

Dove had always finished every bite he was given. He had never not been hungry.

"What's the matter with you?" she chided him. "It's your leg that hurts, not your stomach."

He was down again, and even though she tempted him with carrots and bread, it took her a quarter of an hour to get him up on his feet. Then he did something that brought tears to her eyes. She reached up to comb his mane, and he hung his head over her shoulder and rested it there as if he needed the comfort of leaning on her. He'd nudged and pushed her playfully often enough, but that heavy head had never been slung so pathetically over her shoulder.

"Dove," she implored, "don't give up. We'll get you that operation." She might not be her father, but she must somehow persuade Stella that it was okay to accept the money. No way would Mom allow it if Stella didn't think it was right.

Jan was making little braids in Dove's mane when Stella

appeared in her white uniform. Her long brown hair was in a ponytail and she still sparkled after her day of work.

"Is that the horse all this fuss is about?" Stella asked.

"Hi," Jan said. "Yes, this is Dove."

"He looks kind of droopy."

"His leg is hurting."

"Yeah, that'll do it for sure," Stella said, as if she'd had experience with pain.

"You can come in the corral and meet him," Jan said.

"Not me. I'm scared of horses," Stella said. "Where's your mama? She wanted to have a talk with me about something."

Jan took a deep breath. "It's about Mattie," Jan began. "Mattie gave me a lot of money when she came to our house for supper the other night. And Mom wants to know what you think of letting her lend it to us. It's for an operation for my horse, a really important operation. If he doesn't get it, he could die."

Stella surprised Jan by nodding. "Yeah. I know all about that money, and I have some opinions on it. Why don't you find your mother?"

Stomach churning, Jan ran off to get Mom. Stella had sounded so grim, not at all her usual cheerful self. That must mean she thought it was wrong to keep Mattie's money. And Stella didn't like horses. A cold fist socked Jan in the stomach as she tried to think what she could say to persuade her.

Mom suggested they sit on plastic lawn chairs in the

shade of the tiny ramada because there was more room outside the house than in. She asked Stella if she'd like some iced tea or a soda, but Stella said she was fine.

"I've got to get home and fix my husband's dinner," she said. "He's the kind that doesn't know how to boil water."

Mom smiled. "My husband was the cook in our family."

"Well, they're all good at something or we wouldn't have married them. Right?" Stella said.

Then to Jan's relief, she got down to business, "About Mattie. She asked me for help in pawning her ring. Well, first I told her she shouldn't do it, but she convinced me that, after all, the ring is hers to do with as she likes. It's about the only thing she still has any control over. And she really wants to help Jan and her horse. She's crazy about your daughter, you know."

"It's not just me," Jan said quickly. "Mattie wants to help Dove because she had a horse like him when she was a girl. And she understands. I mean, how important he is."

"Still—" Mom began reluctantly.

"I know. I know," Stella interrupted her. "Anyway, I told Mattie okay. I happen to be friends with the owner of a pawnshop. He went to school with me. And as a favor, he promised he'd hang onto the ring until Mattie can redeem it. The question is, How fast could you repay her? I mean, he can't hold the ring forever, and, you know, Mattie's pretty old." It was Mom to whom Stella had directed her question.

"Today I took a job waitressing a few nights a week,"

Mom said. Jan gasped. Mom frowned at her and addressed her next words to Jan. "I was lucky to get the job. They tell me the tips are good, and I can give Mattie everything I earn there after taxes." Mom looked back at Stella and continued, "But the thing is, it's not right to take money from a person who's not—you know. Does Mattie understand what she's doing?"

"In my opinion, she does—at least about this," Stella said.

"And she's in charge of her own things?" Mom asked. "I'd hate to have anyone saying we wangled a loan from a helpless old lady."

"Well," Stella said, "that's frankly just what her daughter is likely to say if she notices the ring is gone. And that's what worried me at first. But I've been thinking. Why should the daughter get everything if Mattie doesn't want her to have everything? I mean, there's another side to it."

Stella took a deep breath and stared into space, as if she were thinking of how to put it. Finally, she leaned toward Mom and said, "Frankly, Mattie's daughter has been neglecting her lately. Not that Mattie would complain about her precious only child. But my bet is Mattie's privately teed off at her. You know what I mean?"

"Not exactly," Mom said.

Stella twitched her lips comically and rephrased herself. "I think the daughter's done pretty well for herself financially, and she's certainly not straining to make her old mother comfortable. Like she probably could afford to pay for a private room for Mattie, because she's the director of something or other and must get a very good salary. And the cost of a private room wouldn't be that big of a difference every month."

Stella sat back. "I'll tell you, having her own room would make Mattie a whole lot happier."

Jan remembered Mattie's confusion about whether her daughter had an important job or worked at home as a consultant. Stella apparently thought Mattie's daughter still had her job. Jan wondered which was the case.

Meanwhile, Mom was asking Stella, "But does Mattie have the right to give us this loan if the daughter would object?"

"Why not? *Legally*, the ring is still hers," Stella said. "Mattie hasn't been declared incompetent—not yet, anyway. She has a right to do what she wants with her possessions."

Mom turned toward Jan, who looked at her pleadingly. In desperation, Jan said, "If Dad were here, he'd borrow the money. Dad wouldn't make money more important than Dove's life."

Mom winced. "All right," she said. "All right. I still don't like it, but I'll write Mattie an I.O.U. and call the vet tomorrow to schedule the operation."

"Fine," Stella said. "I just hope the daughter doesn't find out the ring is gone. If she got really mad, she could fix Mattie's wagon."

104

"You mean punish her?" Mom asked.

"Um-hmm," Stella said with emphasis.

"Well, then we shouldn't take the money," Mom said.

"Oh, please!" Jan begged in terror as the yes threatened to flip into a no. "We'll pay Mattie back fast."

"You'd better," Stella said. "Listen. Go for it. Mattie'll feel good about saving your horse. And she doesn't have a whole lot to feel good about otherwise." Stella smiled at Jan. "Except having you in her life."

"Thanks," Jan said.

But after Stella left, Jan was more worried than elated. Was her mother strong enough to hold down two jobs when she already got so tired from one? It was terrible to burden Mom this way. And as for her part—leasing Dove out—Jan dreaded it. Even if it was to Lisa, who might be a friend, it was going to put in jeopardy the special bond she felt with Dove. And what if Mattie's daughter found out about the ring and Mattie suffered for her good deed!

The situation was like being stuck in the desert surrounded by cacti. Whether it was cholla, prickly pear, hedgehog, or barrel cactus, whichever way Jan turned, she'd run into thorns.

CHAPTER ELEVEN

On Tuesday, for the first time in weeks, Arizona's bright blue banner of a sky reflected Jan's mood. Mom had called the vet and the operation was set for Thursday. Everything was going to be all right now, Jan promised herself as she finally went to thank Mattie for the contents of the rectangular box and to take her the I.O.U. Mom had signed. Mattie was sitting alone on the back patio with her head propped on her fist when Jan found her.

"Hi, Mattie," Jan said. "I'm sorry I took so long to thank you for lending me that money, but I didn't know if I could keep it and— Are you all right?"

"Umm, today's not such a good day, but I'm okay. What did you say?"

Jan repeated her thanks and her excuse for not coming sooner.

"Oh, that's all right, dear," Mattie said. "I knew you'd

come when you weren't so busy with school and your horse and all." Absently, she rubbed her bare finger where the ring had been as if she missed its weight.

"Well, anyway, now Dove can get the operation he needs," Jan said. "I mean, thanks to you."

Mattie nodded. "An operation. That was what the money was for, wasn't it?" Her eyes seemed glazed as she raised them to look at Jan. "You be sure to come tell me how it goes," she said.

Jan promised she would. "Is something hurting you?" she asked Mattie.

"My head," Mattie said. "I get these spells, but don't you worry. I'll be better soon."

"I hope so," Jan said. She told Mattie about the one-pot dinner she'd made for her mother from soup and beans and tuna fish. "Mom said it was delicious," Jan said and laughed. Mattie laughed with her, but without pleasure. For once, she didn't seem to want to talk.

"Well, I guess I'll let you rest, and come back another day," Jan said.

"Yes, dear, that would be nice," Mattie said. She closed her eyes and dropped her chin on her hand, and Jan left.

On Thursday morning, Jan wanted to stay home from school, but Mom pointed out that even if they followed the horse van that was to take Dove to the animal hospital, all they could do there was wait.

"They're not going to let us stay with Dove. We're better off keeping busy instead of sitting around chewing our nails," Mom said. Reluctantly, Jan had to agree, more because she knew her mother couldn't afford to waste time in the waiting room of an animal hospital than for her own sake.

That day, Jan's math class was working on word problems. She kept making mistakes. She couldn't concentrate, even though math was her best subject, or, at least, the one where she got her best grades. Her mind kept returning to what Dove was doing. Would he go up the ramp into the van without a fuss? He moved so reluctantly lately. Would he move at all for anyone but her?

Of course, Mom would be there when they came for him. Mom could get any horse to do anything. Even horses that had been abused by previous owners and shied away from people would let Mom handle them. It was as if they could sense her gentleness and trusted her. Yes, Jan told herself. She was being vain to imagine that Dove would only behave himself for her. Good-tempered as he was, any reasonably capable horse person could handle him.

Still, he might be scared. Horses were when something unexpected happened. She had spent an hour with Dove before school explaining to him that whatever strange things were done to him would be for his own good. Soon enough he'd be back home and his leg would start to heal. Of course, he probably hadn't understood what she was telling him, and even if, by some miracle, he had, he'd want her there for reassurance. She wished she were with him now.

"You look like something's wrong with you," Lisa said to her in the hall on the way to social studies.

"My horse is getting operated on today."

"But I thought you wanted the operation."

"Yes, but what if it doesn't go right?"

"Oh, come on, Jan. He'll do great. My grandpa had open-heart surgery last month and he's doing fine."

"Horses are delicate."

"So are grandfathers."

Jan had to laugh. "I'm sorry," she said. "I'm glad your grandpa's okay."

"Me, too. I'm nuts about the guy. Do you have grandparents you're close to?"

"No," Jan said, thinking of her grandmother in England. Then she remembered Mattie. "But I have a sort of grandmother-friend I'm close to."

"A grandmother-friend? What's that?" Lisa asked.

"She's a special person who lives near me. When you come over, I'll introduce you to her."

The minute Jan got home from school, she rushed to her mother in the barn.

"I called," Mom said. "They say Dove did well and the operation was a success. He'll be there overnight. Then a couple of days after he gets home, you'll have to start making him walk to exercise the leg. It may be three months until you can ride him."

"But he didn't act up any?"

"Dr. Foster said he was a perfect gentleman. And it's over, Jan. He'll be okay."

Jan nodded, so relieved she felt dizzy. "I'll go tell Mattie. She'll want to know."

"Jan, wait," Mom said. "I'm leaving at four for that waitressing job. That means you'll have to take care of your own supper. And could you—?"

"Feed and water the horses? Sure, Mom. Be glad to," Jan said.

"I'll be working Thursdays through Sundays."

"I'm really sorry, Mom," Jan said fervently.

"About what?"

"That you should have to do two jobs."

"No, that's all right. Waiting tables is different from what I do by day, and I'm no good at sitting still, anyway."

On a sudden impulse, Jan hugged her mother. "Thanks for being so good to me," she said.

Mom didn't hug back, but she didn't pull away, either. "Mattie's the one who deserves the thanks," Mom said. "I'm your mother, but she's just a friend. You tell her we'll have her ring back by next summer."

"It'll take that long?"

"Oh, yeah," Mom said. "You don't get rich quick by

110

doing anything I know how to do." She grinned. "Not that getting rich was ever something I cared about."

"Me, either," Jan said.

"Well, your father always said that money's a great problem solver," Mom said, "but he never let it worry him that we didn't have any."

"*You* worry, though, and I know you didn't want Dove. I never thought I meant that much to you that you'd do all this just for me," Jan said. "I mean, Dad—I know you loved Dad, but—"

Mom raised her eyebrows in surprise. "Why, Jan," she said. "You're my only child. I don't have anyone or anything that means more to me than you." She turned and picked up a bucket as if embarrassed by what she'd said.

Jan stood still, tingling with emotion. Her mother had never come so close to saying she loved her. Not that Jan needed to hear the words now. Mom had proved her love convincingly enough.

Mattie was coming out the back door of the big house when Jan arrived. "I was just going for a walk," Mattie said. Today she was acting like her usual perky self. "Wasn't anybody wanted to come with me, so I set out by my lonesome. Want to keep me company?"

"I'd be happy to." Jan offered Mattie her arm. Mattie took and squeezed it.

"Oh, it's so nice to see you," Mattie said. "How are you doing?"

"Fine, but what I wanted to tell you—Dove had his operation today."

"Your horse? He had an operation? Oh, my! And how's he feeling?"

"Well, he's still in the hospital, but Mom called the vet and she says he's doing fine. He may be home tomorrow."

"Hot diggity! That's what my daddy used to say when he got good news. Hot diggity!" Mattie laughed. "Won't it be wonderful to see that pretty horse kicking up his heels!"

"Thanks to you."

"Oh, I didn't do anything much."

"Yes, you did, Mattie. You saved Dove."

"Well, if I did, I'm glad."

They walked down the dirt road through the ranch and farther, past the other ranch properties that bordered the road. Mattie was talking about her grandfather's farm and the two old workhorses on it. "They were always harnessed side by side. Even out of harness, they moved like they were attached. They were like Siamese twins, those two. Looked all knobby-kneed and swaybacked, but strong still."

"How long did they live?"

"Oh, until they were thirty-something. But wouldn't you know it? They died within days of each other. My grandpa didn't get workhorses to replace them. He was using a tractor by then. Actually, I suppose, those horses had been eating more than they were worth, but I cried when they died. It was like a piece of my childhood was gone."

"Dove's most of my childhood," Jan said.

"Yes, I know he is." Mattie patted her arm.

On the way back, Jan asked hesitantly, "Have you seen your daughter lately?"

"Uh-huh. Valerie stopped by the other night. She didn't look good, sort of puffy and bags under her eyes, but first thing she asked was where the ring was. My daughter's a sharp one. Doesn't miss a thing."

Jan stiffened. "So what did you say?"

Mattie giggled. "I told her I'd mislaid it. I've mislaid it before. She went looking in the bathroom and all over my dresser and even took the bed apart. I told her it would surely turn up."

"She was upset?"

"Umm. She wanted me to give her that ring when she graduated from college, but my husband said no, he'd bought it for *me*." Mattie stumbled and Jan caught her and held onto her arm.

"My daughter went to college, you know," Mattie said after she'd thanked Jan. "I never did. Girls didn't go that often when I was young, even though my daddy could have sent me, but I was never any brain. Well, and I never worked for pay like my daughter, either. She's got a real important job."

Mattie shook her head as if to clear it. "I don't know why I keep forgetting," she said. "Valerie quit that job last spring, right after she moved me into the home."

She tilted her head as if she were thinking about something. "It was strange," Mattie said. "First, Valerie told me that she couldn't take good care of me—even though I was the one got dinner on the table every night. And I kind of thought I was taking some care of *her.* Then she up and quits her job when there's nobody home to take care of but herself. Can you figure that one out?"

Jan took a deep breath and dared to ask, "Was she angry when she saw you didn't have the ring?"

"Oh, she had something to say all right. Said she can't believe how careless and forgetful I've become. I told her most of the other old ladies in that house were a lot worse off. Anyway, she put up a sign on the bulletin board in the kitchen. 'Substantial reward for return of emerald ring.' That's 'cause she thinks one of the part-time girls took it. Of course, *we* know where it is." Mattie giggled.

"But what if she finds out somehow?"

"How? I hid the pawn ticket good. That and the I.O.U. paper your mother signed. You'll never guess where."

"Where?" Jan asked.

Mattie was eager to tell her. "In my closet in my high-heel silver shoes that I wore once and never got a chance to wear again. Now, as old as I am, I'd break my neck in them. I should give them away, but they're so pretty. It's fun to take them out and look at them. It makes me remember being young."

"It sounds like you found a good hiding place," Jan said with relief.

"I thought so," Mattie agreed.

Jan told Mattie about her mother's waitressing job.

"I'm sorry she's got to take on more work."

"Me, too," Jan said. "But I'm going to do the evening watering and feeding of the horses for her."

"That's nice," Mattie said. "You're such a good girl. I'm lucky to have a granddaughter like you."

Jan was so startled by the slip, she blurted out, "I'm not your granddaughter, Mattie."

"No, no, I know that." Mattie looked confused. "I meant, if you *were* my granddaughter . . . I always wanted my daughter to get married and have children, but she never did, and now she's past fifty. Well, anyway." Mattie shook her head yet again, as if she were trying to clear it. "Oh, me," she said. "Some days my mind's in such a muddle."

That admission frightened Jan. Quietly, she asked, "Mattie, what's my name?" Because the thought that Mattie never used it had leaped out of the back of Jan's mind.

"Your name? Why, it's— I know it, of course. You're my friend. But—it's hard to remember names. Lots of people can't remember names, you know."

Mattie settled her feathers soon enough, but Jan remained disturbed. She'd discomforted her friend—and worse than that, it seemed that Mattie really didn't always know what she was doing.

CHAPTER TWELVE

"Dove!" Jan yelled joyfully as she ran toward his corral Friday afternoon after school. There he stood with his head held high, ears perked toward her, and his eyes alive with interest again. The only bad thing was that he was still standing on three legs. His right front leg was thickly wrapped in bandages.

"How are you feeling?" she asked him. "Better? You're going to feel much, much better soon. And before you know it, you and I'll be trail riding again. We might even get Mom to trailer you over to Sabino Canyon to ride there. Wouldn't that be fun?"

She fussed over him, scratching the underside of his jaw and brushing his mane, checking his hooves for dirt. But she didn't find any. They'd sent him home from the hospital in good shape.

Except that he didn't seem to want to use his leg.

116

For the next three days, Jan rushed to Dove's corral as soon as she got up, only to find him standing in the tripod position. He was lively from ears to body, but reluctant to move his feet even to get to treats. She kept trying to follow doctor's orders and walk him, but Dove seemed convinced that he was a three-legged horse. He *acted* like a three-legged horse as he hobbled reluctantly along while she tugged at his lead. She coaxed him with words and with treats, and even, when she got frustrated, with scoldings, but he stubbornly refused to use his right front leg.

"You want me to get behind you and push?" she asked him. "Wouldn't that look silly? Wouldn't you be embarrassed?"

He muttered at her obligingly, but whether he was agreeing or not, the result was the same. She was still trying to figure out how to make him put weight on his right front leg on Thursday when Lisa came home from school with her. Lisa's parents had said they might consider letting her lease a horse as a Christmas present, since Mom had quoted them a reasonable price.

"So I'd better meet Dove to see if he's the right horse for me," Lisa had said.

"Well, you can't ride him for months or maybe never, the way he's acting," Jan told her. "Mom says he probably expects it to hurt if he puts any weight on the leg that got fixed."

"I still want to meet him," Lisa had said.

The two girls had gone straight from the bus stop to Dove's corral.

"Boy, he's big," Lisa said when she saw Dove. "I guess moving him is like the joke about letting a two-ton gorilla sit wherever he wants. I mean, you can't pick him up. Unless you had a crane or something. What are you going to do?"

"Beats me. I've run out of ideas," Jan said. "You don't have any, do you?"

"How about if you scared him?"

Jan looked at Lisa doubtfully. "Well, we could try it."

The only scary thing Jan could think of was banging on a metal pail. She found one in a corner of the barn. If she hit it with a shovel, it should clang loud enough to spook even a horse as unflappable as Dove.

"We'd better try it in the arena, where he's got more room to run," Jan said. It took a while for her to get Dove to hobble into the arena. She had Lisa follow with the pail and shovel, staying back behind Dove, where he couldn't see her. At Jan's signal, Lisa banged away so loudly that horses' heads appeared over pipe fences and out barn stall windows all over the ranch. Dove, however, merely looked calmly over his shoulder to get a better view of the pail.

A horse neighed as if asking what was going on. Jan had to laugh as Dove nonchalantly pushed at the pail with his nose, still careful not to put any weight on his right front foot.

"I guess he's not very scareable," Lisa said.

"No, that's one of the good things about him. He doesn't spook easy."

Jan remembered that she'd asked her mother to buy some

watermelon. Watermelon rind was one of Dove's favorite treats, and he never got any out of season when it became expensive. She took Lisa back to the casita. Sure enough, Mom had stowed a small hunk of plastic-wrapped watermelon in the refrigerator. Lisa looked around the tiny kitchen and living room space without commenting.

"Want some watermelon?" Jan asked.

"No, save it for Dove if he likes it so much," Lisa said. "Where do you sleep?"

"With my mother."

"I have my own room," Lisa said.

"You're lucky," Jan said.

"No, you are. You have your own horse," Lisa said. They both laughed and returned to the arena. When they tried to tempt Dove with the rind, he tossed his head and hopped toward them eagerly on three legs.

Disgusted, Jan climbed up the pipe rail fence and flopped forward over it like a rag doll.

"What's with you?" Lisa asked. "If you're trying to hang yourself, you're wrong end up."

"Very funny," Jan said. "I just don't know what to do with him." She stood straight up on the round bottom rung with her back toward Dove. "I could try lying down and playing dead," she said. "One time when Dove and I were trail riding, I took a rest by a stream, and Dove came over to sniff me. I guess he wanted to see if I was still alive."

"Now you're going to lie down in the *dirt* for that dumb

horse that doesn't know he's cured? What if he decides to use your chest as a footrest?"

Lisa was right. It wouldn't be safe to risk having Dove step on her. "Well, you think of something, then," she said in frustration.

Lisa climbed the fence and sat on the top rail next to Jan. "When do I get to meet this grandmother-friend of yours?"

"Mattie? We could go over there and see her anytime. She's always at home. Unless she takes a walk. And then she might stop by here." It occurred to Jan that she hadn't seen Mattie since she'd gone over to report that Dove's operation had been a success. Mattie had said she was coming by when Dove got back from the hospital, but she hadn't come. Why not? Jan asked herself.

She was about to suggest they go to the big house right away when Lisa whispered, "Stay still. He's coming."

Sure enough Dove was ambling toward them, a three-legged amble, but at least he was moving on his own. He stretched his neck out and sniffed at the back of Jan's head.

"Now what? You think I stink?" Jan asked him over her shoulder.

Dove jerked his head up and did his lip-curling grin.

"I know my hair needs washing," Jan said. "But I didn't think it was that bad."

Lisa giggled and said, "You and that horse are a comedy team. I didn't know horses could smile."

"Horses are a lot more human than you'd think by

looking at them," Jan said. She climbed down off the fence and pulled off Dove's halter. "I might as well leave him out here while we go see Mattie. He might forget about his leg and start moving by himself."

"I wouldn't bet on it," Lisa said. But it was worth a try and an easy thing to do.

On the way to the big house, Jan described the women who lived there. "They're really old, but they're still people, you know? I mean, just because they're old doesn't mean they're not like us anymore. I mean, they're not like you and me exactly, but—"

"But what?" Lisa was frowning.

"Well, they're individuals," Jan finished lamely.

"Isn't everybody?" Lisa asked.

Jan couldn't think of a reply to that. It shamed her to remember that not so long ago she hadn't thought of the very old as individuals.

Amelia was sitting in the shade of the ramada with her face turned to the mountains quite as if she could still see them. "That's Mattie's roommate," Jan whispered to Lisa. "She's mostly blind."

When they were standing in front of Amelia, the old woman turned toward them inquiringly. Jan said, "Hi, Amelia. Remember me? I'm Mattie's friend, Jan. I'm here with a girl from my class in school. She came to meet my horse." Amelia's blindness obliged Jan to fill in the picture with words. She stopped and waited awkwardly for a response.

Amelia said, "Hello, there. Are you here to see Mattie?"

Jan nodded, then remembered and said, "Yes."

"Well, she's gone. They took her to the nursing home." From the gloom in Amelia's tone, it sounded as if she'd said Mattie had been taken to a funeral home.

Jan gasped. "No!"

"Last weekend. She didn't get to take her things. I suppose they'll come back for them. I'm alone in the room now—for a while, anyway."

"But, Amelia, why did— What happened? Did she get sick or something?" Jan asked.

"You'll have to ask Stella. Nobody tells me anything." Amelia took out a tissue and blew her nose. "About the only thing Mattie and I agreed on was we had to keep out of that place somehow. I don't know what happened to her. All I know is they took her away." Suddenly, Amelia's cheeks crumpled and her long, thin fingers flew to screen her face.

Jan reached out to touch her shoulder in sympathy, but the tall woman shook her off in an unspoken wish to be left alone.

Quietly, Jan led Lisa into the house to look for Stella. Another attendant was there instead, an owlish lady who said she was new and that she was filling in for Stella, who'd taken a day off. When Jan asked her what had happened to Mattie, the woman said, "I don't know one of them from the other yet." Again she said, "I'm new."

"What are you so upset about?" Lisa asked as they

walked away from the big house. "You look like you're going to cry."

"I've got to get Mattie out," Jan said. "It's my fault she's there. Her daughter thinks Mattie's gotten senile now because Mattie told her she lost the ring."

"I don't get you," Lisa said.

"If you're really mental or half dead, they put you in the nursing home, and then you die," Jan said. "At least that's what Amelia and Mattie think happens."

"So your grandmother-friend's dying?"

"Not if I get to her fast enough," Jan said. "I'll make them let me take her home with me. Mom will understand. We can get a folding cot and fix it up for her at night in the living room."

"Yeah, I'll bet!" Lisa said as if she thought Jan was dreaming.

But later, with Lisa standing silently beside her in the shed where Mom was hanging up bridles, Jan told her mother what had been done to Mattie. "Could we bring her to live with us?"

Mom chewed her lip for a minute, then said, "Well, we don't have any room or any time or any money, but . . . Seems like we ought to do something if we're the cause of her trouble. Let me think about it."

"Maybe I should tell Mattie's daughter what really happened to the ring and that we're going to get it back," Jan said.

"Before we do anything," Mom said, "we had better go over to that nursing home and see what's what."

"Let's go right now."

"No," Mom said. "Right now I've got to go help the farrier shoe our prime boarder. He can't handle that horse alone. We'll go tomorrow."

"I'll stay home from school so we can go in the morning," Jan said.

"No, you won't," Mom said. "I can't leave the ranch until I finish my morning chores. What we'll do is, I'll pick you up at school after your lunch hour, and we'll go from there."

"But how do you know which nursing home she's in?" Lisa asked.

"It's got to be the one that's owned by the same organization that bought our house," Mom said. "It's where their head office is, near the old shopping mall in the middle of Tucson."

Lisa's mother honked for her from the dirt road. "I've got to go, Jan," Lisa said. "I'll see you in school. Meanwhile, if I can do anything, call me."

"Thanks, Lisa," Jan said. "I'm sorry today was such a mess."

"What do you mean? This is the most excitement I've had in weeks. I like your horse. And good luck tomorrow. Bye, Mrs. Wright." Lisa waved and ran for the car, where her mother was again tooting the horn for her.

First Dove and now Mattie, Jan thought. Was everyone

who mattered most to her taking turns falling apart? She called the nursing home that night. When she asked to speak to Mattie, she was told Mattie had no phone in her room and couldn't leave her bed. "Is she sick?" Jan asked.

"What is your relationship to the patient?" the cool voice asked.

"I'm her friend."

"Sorry," the woman said. "We're not at liberty to give out information about our patients except to the immediate family."

Next time she called, Jan decided, she'd claim to be Mattie's granddaughter. It wouldn't be much of a lie. She was beginning to feel as if she really was.

CHAPTER THIRTEEN

Somehow, Jan endured the stretched-out minutes of the next school day. At a quarter of two, her mother's note about the "appointment" they had to keep allowed her to escape from the building. Mom was waiting for her in the old pickup truck across the street.

"I called Mattie's daughter. Stella gave me the telephone number," Mom said.

"So what did you find out?"

"First of all, Stella told me Mattie's in the nursing home because she fell."

"Oh." Jan breathed a sigh of relief. "Then it's okay? She'll be going back to the assisted living home?"

"Well, that's not what the daughter said. She said Mattie's been having a lot of trouble lately, that she's getting forgetful and isn't doing well. She wanted to know why we were interested. I told her I was your mother and that you

were Mattie's friend. She said Mattie had talked about you."

"Did she sound . . . nice? The daughter?"

"Hard to say. She was kind of cautious, like she wasn't going to trust a stranger right off the bat. But she was polite."

"Mattie's not getting forgetful, not *that* forgetful, anyway," Jan said. "Her daughter just thinks that because of the ring—because Mattie had to say she lost it. I've got to tell her daughter what really happened."

"Better make sure that's what Mattie wants first," Mom said.

They had arrived at the parking lot next to the three-story adobe-style building with its discreet nursing-home sign. Mom parked the truck and asked, "Want me to go in with you?"

Jan studied the boxy building with distaste. Bathed in a harsh midday sun under a clear November sky, it had all the cheerfulness of a bleached bone. She dreaded entering it alone, but she made herself say, "That's okay. I can do it."

"Well, I could use the time to buy supplies." Mom waited a beat. "You sure?"

Jan hesitated. Having Mom with her would shield her from whatever awful things were inside that place which Mattie and Amelia feared. But the least she owed Mattie was some courage. "I'll be okay," she said finally. "I just have to go in and ask to see her, right?"

127

Mom nodded. "It's visiting hours. And you don't need to be a relative. I called and asked."

"And you'll pick me up back here in an hour or so?"

"An hour," Mom said. "I've got to be at the restaurant on time. Wait here in the parking lot for me." Mom's eyes assessed her. "You'll do all right, Jan," she said. "You'll do fine."

Mom's reassurance gave Jan the jump start she needed. She turned her back on the truck, marched to the front entrance, and waited while the doors slid open. A receptionist sat at a desk in the bare, saltillo-tiled lobby. The only other person there was slumped in a wheelchair. The person, a woman, Jan guessed by the housedress, looked as nearly dead as Jan had expected.

She shivered and gave her name to the receptionist, who said Mattie was up on the third floor in room 312. With her pen, she pointed the way to the elevator.

When Jan pressed the elevator button, the old woman in the wheelchair startled her by speaking without lifting her head from her chest. "Take me to four."

The elevator doors opened. "Roll me in," the old woman commanded in a deep masculine voice.

Jan was about to obey when the receptionist called to her, "Just leave her be. She likes to roam. We don't have a fourth floor here."

"Sorry," Jan whispered to the wheelchair-bound lady. She stepped into the elevator and pressed the top number, three. The old woman glared right at her, as if Jan had betrayed her. Jan's heart was pounding and her throat felt dry. She swallowed and said again, "Sorry." Finally, the elevator door closed against the accusing eyes.

When the elevator reached three, Jan stepped out into a bare beige corridor lined with rooms whose doors stood open to reveal the most decrepit people she had ever seen. It was every bit as depressing as she had imagined. Barely living lumps of helpless humanity lay on beds or sat in chairs. She spotted a nursing station down the hall, and headed for it quickly, trying not to look into the rooms as she passed them. Though the vinyl-tiled floor seemed clean, a faint odor of urine hung in the air. Somebody was groaning. A toothless man, pushing a metal stand with plastic attachments hanging from it, shuffled past her in his bathrobe.

Just before she reached the nursing station, Jan spotted room number 312 out of the corner of her eye. With relief, she ducked into it. And there was Mattie. She looked incredibly small lying in bed, covered to her chest by a sheet. Her eyes were closed, and her hair was stuck together in wisps on her pale scalp. Trembling, Jan approached her.

"Mattie," she said. "Mattie. It's me, your friend, Jan."

Mattie's eyes opened. She squinted at Jan with a pained expression as if she didn't know who she was. Then she sighed and smiled. "Oh, hi, honey. What're you doing here?"

"Visiting you."

"Where am I, then? I don't know this place. It scares me."

"Well, it's sort of a hospital," Jan said. "But you'll get out of here as soon as you're well."

"I'm sick?"

"They said you fell."

Mattie thought about it. "I don't remember. But my bottom hurts. I can't move it too well. You say I fell?"

"That's what I heard."

"Well, that'd explain it, then. How long do I have to stay here?"

"I don't know. Until your bones knit back together, I guess. Want me to ask someone?"

"Not now. Don't leave me. It does me good just to see your sweet face. You're such a pretty girl."

"Mattie, I'm not. I'm too tall and my face is too long."

"Now, you telling me I can't see well anymore, either?" Mattie asked with a return of her old spunk. "You're *supposed* to smile and say thank you when someone gives you a compliment." Mattie reached out her small hand and Jan closed her fingers around it. The hand felt so dry and fragile that Jan feared it would break if she squeezed too hard.

"So, now, how's your horse doing?" Mattie asked.

"The vet says the operation was a success and Dove should be fine, but I can't get him to walk. He probably still thinks his leg'll hurt him if he puts weight on it."

Mattie chuckled. "I know just how he feels. You tell him I asked after him and give him a pat for me, hear?"

"I will."

"He'll be all right," Mattie added. "He's not going to stand around on three legs forever, not young as he is."

"I hope not."

"And I'm here because . . . ?"

"Because you fell."

"But I'm not going to stay?"

"No. Even if your daughter doesn't— Well, I think Mom will let you come live with us if it doesn't work out for you to go back to the big house. Like if they get another roommate for Amelia or something," Jan fabricated quickly.

"Oh, Amelia. She ask about me?"

"She doesn't know what happened to you except they took you away."

Mattie smiled and said, "Yes, she probably expects I'm as good as dead. That Amelia always thinks the worst."

Jan laughed. It was true Amelia was something of a pessimist.

"Well, I'll come visit you as much as I can until you get well enough to leave here," Jan promised. "But don't expect me every day because I have to get someone to drive me, and you know how busy Mom is."

"Don't you worry about it. I'll be fine now that I know you're waiting for me. But, honey, one thing we've gotta do."

Mattie made as if to sit up in bed. A spasm of pain crossed her face and she squeezed her eyelids shut for a minute. Jan made a sympathetic sound. She could feel the pain reflected in her own bones. Mattie opened her eyes and said, "It's okay. Just whatever I broke hurts some. But listen, what I want to say is—" She hesitated and seemed to be searching inside her head.

"We have to do something," Jan said.

"Oh, right. You have to go to my room and get those papers out of the silver shoes. Do it before my daughter finds them. Or she'll be real mad at me."

"You mean the paper from the pawnshop?"

"And the one from your mother. You keep them for me. Don't lose them. We need that pawn ticket to get back my ring."

"Mattie, wouldn't it be best to tell your daughter what really happened?"

"No, no, no! You mustn't tell her. If you do, she'll say I'm not responsible. Anyone can lose something, but if she knows I gave it away—" Mattie took a deep breath. "Just do like I say."

"Okay," Jan said. "I'll go to the house and see if they'll let me into your room. I'll tell them you asked me to bring something to you at the nursing home."

"That's right. Stella will let you. Stella's partial to me."

The hour passed quickly. It was easy to talk to Mattie, even here in this place. She was either reminded of a story to tell or she asked questions. When it was time for Jan to leave, she realized she'd had Mattie's hand in hers the whole time. The hand was warm and felt more alive now.

She bent and kissed Mattie's forehead. "I'll come back as soon as I can," Jan promised.

"I'll be waiting for you," Mattie said. "It'll give me something to look forward to. Thanks for coming, honey."

"My name's Jan," Jan said.

"I know who you are. I know. It's just your *name* I can't remember," Mattie said.

"Lots of people aren't good at names," Jan said.

"Well, I used to be," Mattie admitted. "When I was young, I was good at remembering. There's a lot of things I was good at that I can't do right anymore." She smiled. That was something Mattie could still do beautifully, Jan thought.

"How is she?" Mom asked when Jan got back into the truck.

"She doesn't like it there. But she was very glad to see me."

They agreed that Mom would drive Jan to the nursing home three times a week until Mattie got out. Mom said she would try to find out when that would be.

"I've got to get something for her from the house," Jan said.

Mom didn't ask what the something was and Jan decided not to tell her. Mom might think it was like stealing or something to take those papers from where Mattie had hidden them. Actually, it *was* like stealing, and Jan had never taken anything that wasn't hers in her entire life. But this was a crime for a good cause, and it was a very small crime and a very important cause. She could do it, she assured herself. She *had* to do it.

CHAPTER FOURTEEN

Getting into Mattie's room in the assisted living home turned out to be easy. Stella opened the front door while holding a telephone receiver to her ear. She put her hand over the receiver and asked Jan, "Did you get to see Mattie in the nursing home?"

"I just came from there."

"Good! I meant to visit her myself, but I haven't made it yet. How's she doing?"

"Okay, I guess. She wants me to bring her something from her room."

"Oh, all right, then. You go ahead and I'll talk to you later." Stella waved Jan in and resumed talking into the phone.

Jan passed two women she didn't know in the living room and glimpsed Amelia sitting out on the back patio. Quietly, she opened the door and stepped into Mattie and Amelia's shadowy bedroom. When Mattie was present, it hadn't seemed polite to examine this room, which had been Jan's private sanctuary for so many years. Now that she was alone in it, she gave in to the urge to find some trace of her past self. But with two partial sets of mismatched furniture crammed into it, the room resembled a furniture store more than a secret retreat.

Jan opened the closet door to find her name just where she had carved it above the doorknob. But it struck her as sad, like a name carved on a gravestone. Nothing else remained of her here, even though she'd been gone less than a year.

One deep breath and she turned to the job at hand. First, she had to determine which side of the big closet was Mattie's and which was Amelia's. Mattie was small; Amelia was tall. All right, but the clothes were jammed so tightly on the rod that it was hard to tell sizes. Below the hanging garments were shoeboxes next to a rack full of shoes that had to be too big to be Mattie's. In a row on top of the boxes were child-size shoes. Mattie's, then. But no silver slippers.

Jan crouched to study the end panels on the boxes. Which one should she open first? She'd make a terrible private investigator, she told herself. This whole business made her feel sneaky. Gingerly, she lifted the top of first one box and then the other. Finally, she located the silver sandals— high-heel, sling-back sandals that were indeed glamorous. She was about to poke through the tissue paper in the box for the papers when she heard a noise. Her heart leaped. Caught in the act!

"I'm in the closet, Stella," Jan made herself say. It had to be Stella come to see what she was up to.

The closet door behind her creaked as it was opened wide. "Who are you?" a cold voice asked.

Jan jumped up in guilty terror, hiding the shoe behind her. She was facing a grim-faced middle-age woman with gray hair clipped very short. The woman was primly dressed in a straight skirt and striped blouse.

"I'm Jan, Mattie's friend. I came to get her something."

"And what might that be?"

"Who are you?" Jan dared to ask.

"I'm her daughter, Valerie Williams."

"Oh," Jan said. "Oh." She swallowed and gazed in dismay at Mattie's daughter.

"What are you after?" Valerie Williams demanded.

Jan had never been a good liar. She blurted out, "Mattie said she wanted . . . her silver shoes."

"You mean what was hidden in them, don't you?"

In a flash, Jan understood why she hadn't immediately seen the papers in the slippers. "How did you find them?" she asked.

"I was looking for the ring. My mother said she'd lost it again, so I did a thorough search of her things while I was getting her a nightgown for the nursing home."

Hastily, Jan began to explain. "Mattie hocked her ring for me. My horse needed an operation. My mother's working nights. And I'm going to lease my horse. We'll repay the

137

money, and Mattie'll get the ring back. By next summer, my mother says."

"I've already redeemed the ring." The daughter held her hand out so that Jan could see that she was wearing it. "I'm the one you'll have to repay." Valerie narrowed her eyes. "Give me your name and address and telephone number. I need to talk with your mother about this business," she said.

Jan didn't like the sound of that. Stiffly, she said, "Mom's working two jobs to pay you back. My mother's very honest." And then she asked the question that had been haunting her. "Was that why you made Mattie go to the nursing home? Because she said she lost the ring?"

"You think I punished my mother?" Valerie's eyebrows shot up in surprise.

Jan didn't know what to answer, and with Valerie blocking her way out of the closet, she felt trapped. If only her father were there! He would know what to say to Mattie's suspicious daughter. No doubt he'd be careful not to make Valerie lose her temper by accusing her of anything. He'd just give her the facts calmly. He used to say you could get through most anything with horses and people if you kept it soft and easy.

"Well, you didn't want Mattie in your house anymore," Jan began slowly. "And then you don't visit her very much here. So—"

Valerie gasped and her face turned white, as if Jan had shocked her. "You must think I'm some kind of monster!" she said. "Whatever did my mother tell you about me?"

138

Jan took a deep breath and began to pick her way cautiously through what she knew. "All Mattie said was that you were smart," she told Valerie. "She said that you graduated from college and had a good job, but you quit it after you moved her in here. She just doesn't understand why you wanted to get rid of her."

"Wanted to get rid of her?" Valerie made a strangled sound, and her face twisted as if she were in pain. "She couldn't have said that. My mother knows how much I love her."

"You do?" Jan couldn't keep the doubt out of her voice. "Are you going to bring her back here, then? I mean, you're not going to leave her in the nursing home?"

"Of course I'm not," Valerie said.

"Because if you are," Jan put in hopefully, "Mattie could come and live with us. I'm pretty sure my mother would let her, even though we don't have much room."

Abruptly, Valerie sat down on the end of Mattie's bed. "Come on out of that closet," she said. "We need to talk."

Jan stepped into the room uncertainly. Valerie was staring at the coverlet, smoothing the crazy quilt design. Her hands were small and dainty like Mattie's. Otherwise, she didn't resemble her mother. For one thing, Valerie was twice as wide—not more than a few inches taller, but stockier. For another, the lines of her puffy face were drawn down, while Mattie's face seemed designed for smiling.

"If my mother's been complaining that I've neglected

her lately," Valerie began, "I can understand it. But it's not because I wanted to."

"She hasn't been complaining," Jan said. "Only you don't come when you promise, and that makes her feel bad."

"She'd feel worse if she knew what was wrong," Valerie said. The eyes that met Jan's had a wounded look. "My mother and I are so close. We're everything to each other," Valerie said. "And something terrible has been happening to me. I thought it would kill her if she knew."

"If she knew what?" Jan asked.

Valerie studied Jan with care. "How good are you at keeping secrets?" she asked.

"You mean from Mattie?"

"From everybody. I know Stella the manager here thinks I'm a terrible daughter. It's in her tone of voice when I call, and the way she looks at me—I haven't told her, either." Valerie pressed her fingers to her lips.

"Maybe you *should* tell her," Jan said. "And your mother, too."

Valerie eyed Jan thoughtfully. "My mother didn't actually say she thought I didn't love her, did she?"

"She wouldn't say anything bad about you," Jan said. "But she cried once."

"When?"

"When you didn't come for her birthday."

"Oh, her birthday!" Valerie's eyes glistened with tears. "I was so sick that day. I could barely drag myself out of bed,

140

and I brought her a pathetic bunch of flowers because I just couldn't—" The tears slid down her cheeks. "I've had breast cancer," she said. "I set my mother up here so that I could hide from her when I was going through the operation and the chemotherapy and—everything I had to go through."

"Are you okay now?" Jan asked cautiously.

Valerie shrugged. "I'm in remission. That's okay enough, I guess. But I can't believe . . . How could my mother imagine that I'd ever stop loving her? We've always been so close."

"Yeah, she did say that," Jan said.

"Then you understand?" Valerie asked. "The reason I've neglected her? One look at me on some days and she'd have known something bad was happening to me."

Jan nodded and said, "Well, I'm glad. I mean, that you're all right and that you really love her. But why can't you tell her the truth now?"

"I don't know. She's gotten so frail." Valerie rubbed at her forehead and closed her eyes as if she were thinking.

"Because you're not going to die or anything anymore," Jan said.

Valerie laughed. "No. My doctor thinks we may even have licked it."

"And Mattie could use some good news," Jan persisted.

"Everybody can use good news. But she'd be frightened to know how sick I've been. She can't even say the word cancer without shuddering."

"I'm really sorry that I thought you were mean," Jan said.

"Well, I'm not sweet like my mother, that's for sure." Valerie's face lifted in a smile that finally made her resemble her mother. And she said, "You know, my mother talked about you. She told me you were just the grandchild she wished she had. I wanted to give her grandchildren. But— Anyway, I hope you're convinced that I do love and appreciate my mother."

"Sure," Jan said, "I believe you." It was Mattie who still needed to be convinced.

"Okay, then," Valerie said, getting back to business. "For now, would you just tell my mother you hid the papers somewhere for her? I'll show her I've got the ring when the time's right."

Jan nodded.

"And when I pack up her stuff and sort out what to toss and what to save, I'd better keep those silver sandals she's so crazy about, hadn't I?"

"You mean Mattie's not coming back here?" Jan asked in alarm.

Valerie shook her head wearily. "I can't afford to keep paying for this room. Cancer's expensive. I've been trying every cure I hear about, and insurance won't cover what the doctor doesn't prescribe."

"So when she leaves the nursing home—?"

"I'm not sure what'll happen then. Listen, I need time to

think. Would you please just not tell anyone what we talked about here? Will you keep it to yourself for a while and let me decide about telling my mother?"

"Okay," Jan agreed. She had done the best she could, and having talked to Valerie, she trusted that the woman would find a way to make things right.

Stella was nowhere in sight when Jan walked through the house and out the back door. That was a relief. With all the promises and cross-promises Jan had made to both Mattie and her daughter, she didn't want to risk talking to anybody about anything. Still, she returned to the casita in a cheerful mood. Mattie's daughter wasn't a monster, after all, and life seemed suddenly more fair.

Now all she had to do was figure out how to make Dove use his leg again. She found him in his favorite spot under the mesquite tree, leaning sideways to avoid putting weight on his fixed leg.

"Dove," she said, "you'll never believe what I just found out." She put an arm around his long neck, and looking into the intelligent brown eye nearest her cheek, she told him all about it.

CHAPTER FIFTEEN

Two days before Thanksgiving, while Jan was in school, Valerie came to speak to Jan's mother about the money Mattie had lent them. Valerie had been crisp but cordial, according to Mom. They had agreed upon regular monthly payments, and Valerie had left with an initial check. "We should be free of debt by next June, if all goes well," Mom told Jan.

"And you'll quit your waitressing job then?"

"You bet," Mom said with a grin.

The day before Thanksgiving, Lisa came into school beaming. She told Jan that her parents had agreed to let her lease Dove starting in January. "Dad's calling your mother to set it up. Isn't that great?"

"Uh-huh," Jan said. Her stomach lurched briefly at the idea of sharing Dove. She felt as if she had agreed to go shares in a brother or sister, but she reminded herself that this was her contribution toward Dove's recovery.

"That's good," Jan made herself say to Lisa. And she told herself to be glad Dove was being leased by a friend. "Now, how about helping me convince Dove he's cured?"

Lisa hit a jubilant high five with her and said, "Let's do it."

On Thanksgiving day, Mom worked at the restaurant while Jan filled in for her at the ranch. That night, when they were eating the leftover turkey Mom brought home, Jan said, "I guess we have a lot to be thankful for."

"I guess we do," Mom agreed. "Including that I didn't have to cook this." They smiled at each other.

For the next three weeks, Jan and Lisa spent a part of every lunch hour concocting schemes to get Dove to put weight on his healing leg. Lisa wanted to try scaring Dove again. "Because what does a horse do when he's scared?" she asked Jan.

"He runs away."

"Yeah? And can he run on three legs?"

"Not likely," Jan said.

"Okay," Lisa said. "So I'll charge into Dove's corral in that witch costume I wore for Halloween, and you scream, and Dove will run away on all four legs. It's simple."

Jan was doubtful. Deliberately scaring Dove seemed mean. Besides, they'd tried it once and it hadn't worked. But she couldn't come up with a better idea, so she agreed to Lisa's plan.

The next afternoon after school, Lisa brought her Halloween costume home on the bus with Jan and changed into it in the casita. Her dress was full of spangles and trailing scarves that floated eerily in the fitful December wind.

As planned, Lisa sneaked out to Dove's corral, hiding behind Jan so she could jump out and surprise him. But when Jan screamed and Lisa began leaping about and flapping her arms, Dove wasn't fazed. He lowered his head, watching Lisa, then nudged Jan as if to say, "What's with your friend?"

Their next idea was to walk Dove down the slope to the wash. It was hard for him to balance on three legs going up and down, and they hoped he'd need to use his mended leg. But he managed to lurch awkwardly along without it.

On another windy day that week, Lisa brought a bag of balloons. The girls blew up a dozen with much huffing and puffing and set them loose in the arena with Dove. As the crayon-colored balloons flew about, Dove turned to watch. His ears twitched with interest, but he didn't chase a single one.

Next, Jan tried running around the ring just inside the fence. She went around twice, and Lisa joined her on the third go-round. Dove watched them with a mildly perplexed expression, his ears turning as they ran, but not a step did he take to join them.

146

Along with her efforts to get Dove to move, Jan was visiting Mattie in the nursing home three times a week. Her mother took her twice, and on Wednesdays, when Lisa's mother had her weekly hair appointment in that direction, she took both girls. Lisa found an old man named Al who was palsied but still mentally alert enough to enjoy a checker partner. She stayed in the lounge with Al and played checkers while Jan visited with Mattie.

They talked about Dove and his obstinacy. Mattie kept assuring Jan that someday Dove would surprise her and just start using his leg. "You wait and see. It'll happen," Mattie said.

Every so often Mattie would make a remark about her daughter's visits that showed an edge of disappointment. Each time, Jan was tempted to break her promise to Valerie. It seemed wrong that Valerie was still withholding the truth from Mattie. Surely, knowing Valerie had had cancer would hurt Mattie less than believing her daughter had stopped loving her. But Jan's father had taught her that promises had to be kept, even ones she came to regret. And she had learned that lesson well.

One afternoon at a pause in their conversation, she asked Mattie, "So have you seen your daughter lately?"

"Oh, yes, she comes by," Mattie said. "But, you know, she doesn't look right to me. I don't think working at home is good for her." Mattie stopped, frowning. Then she added, "And she's not keeping herself nice like she used to. She's got this awful short haircut. Valerie always had such pretty hair."

"Why don't you tell her you don't like it?" Jan said.

"Oh, I wouldn't hurt her feelings," Mattie said. "She's real sensitive about her looks. Valerie never liked what the mirror showed her. I always tried to tell her she was good looking, but—" Mattie sighed and said, "I guess children don't believe their mothers' compliments. Isn't that so, honey?"

"I'm Jan, Mattie."

"I know, but I forget. You should have met me when I was younger. I was so full of energy. I could whip up a dinner and clean the house and do the garden and still be—" She looked toward the door and her face lit up. Jan followed her gaze and saw Valerie.

"Hello, there," Valerie said to Jan. "I didn't know anyone was here with Mother."

"Just me," Jan said, "but I'm leaving."

"That's okay. You're welcome to stay," Valerie said.

"You know this child?" Mattie asked her daughter.

"We've met. At River Haven."

"Well, isn't that nice," Mattie said. She patted the bed beside her. "Come sit down, honey, and give me a kiss."

"Mother," Valerie said with a look at Jan. "Your young friend here thinks I ought to tell you something, and I've decided it's about time I did." Valerie sat down on the edge of the bed and took Mattie's hand.

Jan said quickly, "I've really got to go now. See you soon, Mattie. Bye." Neither woman seemed to hear her, and she hurried from the room without their noticing. The last thing she wanted was to be there when Valerie revealed her secret. What if Mattie fell apart when she heard her daughter had been ill with cancer? Maybe Valerie had been right to hide it from her.

Whatever possessed Jan to think she knew better than a grown woman with years of experience? What if she'd hurt her grandmother-friend by trying to be more like her father and involving herself in other people's lives?

The next time Jan came to visit, Mattie had progressed from getting around in a wheelchair to walking by herself with the aid of a walker. She greeted Jan in the hall, standing upright but holding on to her folding metal walker.

"There you are, honey. You'll never guess what I found out."

"What?" Jan asked, smiling because Mattie looked and sounded like her old self.

"That daughter of mine! You know why she stuck me in that assisted living place?"

"Why?"

"Because the poor girl was sick and didn't want me to see her suffer. She was trying to save me grief. Isn't that sad? I couldn't believe it when she finally told me. What she must have gone through! And all to save *me* misery!" Mattie shook her head.

"Are you glad she told you?" Jan asked.

"Well, yes, because now she's in remission. Her doctor said so. That means she's cured, doesn't it? Well, maybe not cured, exactly, but anyway she'll be fine. You know what else?"

"What else?"

"When I get out of here, she's taking me back home with her. Isn't that something?"

"That's great, Mattie!" Jan was happy for Mattie's sake and relieved for her own. Squeezing Mattie into the casita would have been hard.

"The doctor said he's going to let me out of here this week. It could even be tomorrow. He figures I can finish recovering on my own now. It's like I got this new lease on life. We both do, my daughter and me."

"That's great," Jan repeated.

All of a sudden, Mattie let go of one side of her walker and grasped Jan's arm. "But now how will we ever get to see each other? I live so far away from you and neither of us drives a car."

Jan's eyes filled with sudden tears. "I guess we can talk on the telephone."

"Oh, there you go!" Mattie patted her arm with one hand while she leaned on the metal walker with the other. "You're so smart. I just knew you'd think of something."

150

Jan was glad for Mattie. Oh, yes, she told herself. She was really glad that things had worked out well for her. But selfishly, she knew she was going to miss her. Even if her grandmother-friend couldn't quite remember her name, she had never failed to make Jan feel good.

CHAPTER SIXTEEN

The saguaro cacti were wrapped in Christmas tree lights, and the malls were full of shoppers buying Christmas presents. The sun beamed as brightly as ever, but sometimes the temperature dropped down near freezing overnight.

Jan and Lisa were hanging on the pipe panel gate of Dove's corral, stroking and scratching him as they talked about what fun it would be to go trail riding together. Jan could exercise a boarder and Lisa could ride Dove—that is, if they could ever get Dove moving on all four legs again.

"He is the stubbornest horse I ever met," Jan said.

"What if he never does walk right again?" Lisa shocked her by saying.

While she was thinking up an answer, Jan heard her name being called by her mother. "You've got visitors," Mom yelled from the open door of the barn where she was working on a horse's hooves.

And there were Valerie and Mattie, leaning on her metal walker, coming toward the corral. "Dove," Jan said. "Look who came to see you!" She unlatched the gate and began leading Dove toward Mattie and her daughter.

Suddenly, Dove tossed his head. He snorted. He heaved himself onto his back legs and resisted, but Jan held onto his lead.

"Stop that, you fool. What's the matter with you? You know Mattie."

Dove whinnied and reared. He came down on his two front legs and twisted out of Jan's grip. Then he ran on all four legs for the barn.

"Dove!" Jan yelled.

"He did it!" Lisa squealed.

Left in the dust of Dove's panicked dash for safety, the girls hugged each other with delight.

"I told you he'd just up and use his legs one of these days," Mattie said. She was still leaning on her gleaming metal walker and grinning.

A minute later, Mom led a trembling Dove out of the barn. "What's got him so scared?" she asked.

Jan fixed her gaze on Mattie.

"The walker!" she said. "I'll bet he's scared of Mattie's walker."

It was, of course, the walker. And it took Dove another fifteen minutes of sniffing and investigating it to decide the weird contraption wasn't a threat to him.

"You've saved my horse twice, Mattie," Jan said.

"That's fair enough," Valerie told her. "My mother told me she'd have given up and died in the nursing home without you."

"She's a good granddaughter, isn't she?" Mattie asked Valerie.

No one corrected her. Instead, Jan put her arms around Mattie and hugged her. Dove nudged them both. He wanted in on the loving. "Oh, you," Jan said and brought his head in to make it a three-way hug.

"Let's see him walk," Mom said.

One tug on his lead line was all it took. Dove followed Jan in a circle around everybody, using all four legs as confidently as if he'd never had a problem with any of them.

"Isn't he a handsome fellow?" Mattie chortled. "Just like my Laddie-lee."

Jan grinned, still walking Dove around his small group of admirers.

"You look as if you just won a horse race, Jan," Lisa said.

"Better than that. I just won my horse," Jan said, and her joy exploded in bubbles of laughter.

She stopped abruptly when she saw her mother's face. "What's wrong, Mom?" Jan asked. Mom looked the way she had at Dad's funeral, as if she were choking on tears.

"Nothing's wrong," Mom said. She turned away and walked back to the barn.

Jan ran after her and caught her arm. "No, tell me," she demanded.

154

"You remind me so much of your father. You're growing up to be just like him, Jan." Mom's voice broke.

"Well, is that good?" Jan asked.

"I'd say so!" Mom said.

"I wish Dad could see how well things turned out," Jan said. "He'd be pleased, wouldn't he?" She felt reluctant to let her mother go, and put her arm around Mom's thin shoulders in a gesture that came naturally.

"Very pleased," Mom said. "You going to try riding Dove now?"

"Can I? It's been so long. You think they'd mind waiting for me?" Jan indicated Lisa and Mattie, who were fussing over Dove at the corral while Valerie seemed to be fussing over her mother.

"You don't have to go far," Mom said. "I'll bring out your tack." She headed for the barn.

Dove was watching Jan as she approached him. His ears were cocked in her direction, and everything in his expressive face was focused on her.

"You guys willing to hang around while I ride Dove down the road a ways?" Jan asked.

"That's what we've been working for, isn't it?" Lisa said.

"It would be a sight for sore eyes, you riding your horse at last," Mattie said. "We can visit a little longer, can't we, Valerie?"

"Of course," Valerie said.

"Okay?" Mom called. She was coming out of the barn draped in everything Jan needed, including Dove's saddle and

155

his old blanket. With Mom helping, Dove was read

time. Jan put her foot in a stirrup and swung onto his

Dove dipped his head and tossed it, prancing a little, as

couldn't wait to get started after so long.

"Now, don't you look wonderful!" Mattie said, and whe

she was talking about Dove or Jan, it didn't matter.

Surrounded by smiles, Jan guided Dove out of his co

and to the road. There she put him from a walk to a trot.

moved with his old friskiness, as if he enjoyed being in mot.

as much as she did. She turned him at the end of the ranch ro

and came back at a canter. His gait was so smooth that Jan fe

as if she were sailing a gentle wind on a flying carpet. She

almost forgotten how wonderful Dove's canter was.

"Can you see him, Dad?" she asked in a whisper as sh

slowed him down for the turn to his corral. "Isn't he beautiful

this horse you gave me? Isn't he fine?"

Laughing for joy, she stopped in front of her audience o

four. They were applauding the performance now. Suddenly

Dove neighed as if he were laughing with her.

"I guess he's healed," Jan said.

"Why, I guess we all are," Mattie said. And it was so.